GW00792403

Photocopies of Heaven

Photocopies of Heaven

fiction

Maurice Suckling

LASTIC
PRESS

This collection copyright © 2006 by Maurice Suckling

All stories previously unpublished.

All rights reserved. No part of this publication may be reproduced, stored in a retrieval system, rebound or transmitted in any form or by any means, electronic, mechanical, photocopying, recording or otherwise, without the prior written permission of the author and publisher. This book is sold subject to the condition that it shall not by way of trade or otherwise be lent, resold, hired out or otherwise circulated without the publisher's prior consent in any form of binding or cover other than that in which it is published.

Disposable Planet text © bbc.co.uk. Reprinted with kind permission.

ISBN-10: 0-9548812-8-1
ISBN-13: 978-0-9548812-8-3

Printed and bound in Great Britain by Biddles, King's Lynn, Norfolk

Cover design by Allison Best
Comic strip drawn by rm* (www.rm-star.com)
Typeset by Andrew Hook

Published by:
Elastic Press
85 Gertrude Road
Norwich
UK

elasticpress@elasticpress.com
www.elasticpress.com

About the author:

Maurice likes how newly photocopied paper is warm.

Dear Tall Poppies,

You are both tall, and poppyish.

I loved your set.

Best wishes, exciting times are afoot...

Maurice

Thank you: Andrew Hook of Elastic Press for his advice and faith; Annie Skinner, Neil Richards, Matt Costello, Ruth Chalmers and Dirk Maggs for their encouragement; Claire Malcolm and all at New Writing North and the support of the Northern Promise Award in 2005; my Mum, brother Laurence and Toby Waterman, for their long-term interest and insights; Ben and Jo for their scoring system out of 10; Gaylie Runciman and Debs Norton for their wonderful enthusiasm, time and abilities on The Amazing Adventures; Allison Best for her brain and the pictures she sees in her head; my other friends and family, for not being cross at not getting a bigger mention.

Table of contents

Part One

Life With A Porn Queen

-------Original Message-------
From: Carl Palmer
Sent: 30 November 2006 23:18
To: Hailey Ridley
Subject: life with a porn queen

There's a guy who goes to see a counsellor and tells him, "I got this great life, I live with a beautiful millionaire porn queen in a big house by the sea in a warm country and the sex is just incredible and she's so imaginative and dirty and inventive and it's just brilliant."

"So, what's the problem," says the counsellor.

"The problem is it's all just meaningless, and I know it is and I can't ever forget it for very long, and I know it's stupid of me and I should just enjoy it, but there you go, and that's what I need your help with."

"Well," says the counsellor, "I think there are a lot of people who feel the same…"

"Yeah," says the man, "but look at her," and he takes out a photo of his live-in porn queen, "plus the sex is just incredible."

Two weeks later the porn queen leaves the guy and he's distraught. Clues point to her having eloped with the counsellor, so he goes to see him. But the counsellor has left his job and his house, left no forwarding address and no one knows where he is.

Years and years later the guy, now an old man, is in a betting shop queue when he recognises his former counsellor.

"Hey," he says, "remember me?" But too many years have passed for him to feel bitter.

"Yes, of course," says the ex-counsellor blithely.

"Ok, look," says the man, "just tell me. Was I right?"

"Oh, yes," says the ex-counsellor, grinning broadly, "the sex; incredible, imaginative and dirty and inventive and..."

The guy cuts him off mid sentence.

"Not that," he says. "I mean the other thing. About how it's all just meaningless. Was I right about that?"

"Oh, I see, yes," says the ex-counsellor, his eyes on the ground. "Yes, you were right. It is."

Then the guy watches as the ex-counsellor walks slowly away and gets into a black convertible parked just outside, driving off with the porn queen in the passenger seat next to him.

What Happened Next?

"Soon as we hit the water we zapped onto another planet where you're born old and grow young, and we lived there from the age of 72 and made sculptures of horses till we got back to 18, which is when we returned here, then bobbed back up to the surface gasping for air."

"No. We just hung in the air for twenty minutes, and one by one, from left to right, we each popped like soap bubbles and disappeared for good."

"No. We froze like that and then cracked like crockery and smashed to the floor, then a stray dog snatched up a piece of my leg between its teeth and ran off with it."

It's my Grannie's *What Happened Next?* photo. She says something different each time you ask. It's blu-tacked to the white wall that needs re-painting above her dressing table mirror. It's just above the photo of granddad in his best shirt and tie, to the left of a postcard of Tynemouth Priory in a watercolour.

In the photo, which is black and white, you can see her and three friends. On the back, in faded blue ink, old style proper fountain pen handwriting, it says *April 16th 1952*. Her 18th birthday. All four of them are jumping in mid air, wearing black swimsuits with a clear sky behind them.

Grannie, who's name is Dorothy, is on the left, thick dark hair, waving her right arm. Next there's Gladys, blonde hair up in the air like static. Next to her there's Ivy, knees up almost to her chin. At the end of the line there's Mavis, with both her arms out. There's a bigger gap between her and the others because she's a little higher and off at an angle like a selected cake slice. Grannie worked in the same market as Gladys and Ivy and Mavis.

They're all smiling so big it looks like their faces will burst.

*

Last year on our last day of school, this is what happened:

We left in Fluffy's car, a duck egg blue Morris Minor with a flip-top roof. We were supposed to leave straight after lunch.

"Where the flip-flop is she? Dozy mare." Holly was undoing her seatbelt.

"No, don't," I said. "She'll be here any second."

"I have to go get her." Holly was already out of the seat and slamming the door.

Fluffy dropped her blonde bobbed head onto the steering wheel. It barely made a sound coz it was covered in light blue fluffy fur. She wore a white fluffy sleeveless jacket and her light brown hair was always fluffy.

"What's she doing?" Fluffy picked her head back up and spun round in her seat. "Why's Holly had to go get her?"

"I don't know." I made my eyebrows go high and tried to make them go round at the edges to make it look like I was telling the truth.

Fluffy countered my eyebrows with a scrunchy brow and a lower pitched voice.

"What's going to happen when Holly comes back round the corner?"

"She's going to be saving Sarah G-String from a herd of slathering zombies. Rev the engine!"

*

We put the roof down. When you put the roof down in Fluffy's car you aren't allowed to say what you're doing or the weather might hear and decide to rain. Today there was only one puffy white cloud in the sky.

"It's gonna be brilliant, isn't it!" Little sprinkles of fairy dust lit up in Fluffy's eyes.

Fluffy was excited about the flashmob on Tyneside she was sure was going to happen. According to the internet. The internet knows all but speaks in riddles. Flashmobs are where people meet at a specific time and place, do something random, then leave.

"There was this one time in London," she said, trying to fix eyes with me, "when everyone played air guitar, and the world champion was there!"

"And what do you think will happen this time?" I tried not to let it show in my voice that she'd told me this a few times before.

Then Holly and Sarah G-String burst round the corner with a herd of slathering Daniel Crewes chasing after them. Holly's red hair flying loose like the tail of a comet and Sarah G-String's blonde ponytail swinging like a crank handle. Daniel Crewes have long scything arms and size 16 feet. There's only one, but he's big enough for a herd.

"Drive! Drive!" shouted Holly, then piled into the back seat. Fluffy swung the door open for Sarah G-String and she half jumped into the front seat. The tyres screeched.

"Hey, you put the top down!" shouted Holly when we were clear.

"Oh well done, Holly Footmouth," shouted Fluffy.

*

It was hard to hear. The wind battered into our ears like an out of tune radio.

It was a forty minute drive to Tynemouth Priory at the coast. Fluffy and G-String were in front, so they were ok behind the windscreen. But me and Holly were in the back so the wind gave us scarecrow hair. We'd duck behind the front seats, occasionally putting our heads up to yell "waaaah" or "waaaaay".

At Tynemouth we parked on the cobbles at the top of the hill.

"So what was all that Daniel Crewe stuff about?" I asked Holly, whilst getting out and trying to harness my black wild woman hair.

Holly slid out feet first – Reverse Caterpillar™ style. First trademarked by her on her 16th birthday.

"Sarah G-String was re-ditching AJ again and I ran over to hurry her up." Holly fiddled with her flip-flops. Sarah G-String and AJ were always breaking up and getting back together. Chances are they'll be the first of us to experience domestic bliss – they're getting all the fights out of the way early on.

"I knocked into the Crewemeister by accident – he dropped his Nintendo DS and became a madman – I put an apology spell on him and all!"

"Was your magic weak?"

She nodded, "my magic was weak."

"Was the DS broken?"

"I guess we'll find out if he follows us here – look at that! He broke my flip-flop!"

Holly took her flip-flops off and carried them in her hands.

"Watch out for glass, then," I said, already looking around for any.

*

"You two going to help with the roof?" asked Sarah G-String, re-tightening her blonde ponytail. Today she was wearing her favourite fluffy pink bra with the bubblewrap skirt and jacket I made for her. There were a few Sarah's in our class with surnames beginning with A, G and M – so she was Sarah G – which, added to her choice of usually semi-visible knickers, morphed into Sarah G-String.

"I've done it," said Fluffy, fastening a catch on the car roof with a loud metallic clunk, which seemed to cue my phone to ring. I thought it was mine. It was G-String's. She had the same *Crazy Frog* ringtone. That's when I realised I'd left my phone at home. So now I'd get stick from my mum. She likes me to have my phone so she knows where I am all the time.

"Elaine!" With a thousand 'a's in it.

"Elaaaaaaaaaine! I told you to take your phone! Are you trying to kill me? You do it on purpose, don't you!"

Apart from teachers, my mum is the only person who still calls me Elaine. When I was 13 I was watching *Xena, Warrior Princess*, season 2, episode 28 – *Girls Just Wanna Have Fun*, where Xena and Gabrielle stop Bacchus and his reign of terror. That's when I realised I also needed a name starting with an X, a name full of dynamism, a name that sounded like the ching of a cold steel blade in the face of the forces of evil, a name a thousand miles away from my boring birth name, given to me by a father I'd not seen for years and a mother who had over-used it so much it had stopped sounding human. What I needed was the name of Xena.

My mum's thing is bad moods. She doesn't like the way her life turned out or the job she does or the men she meets. I'm the person she takes it out on because there's no one else.

I thought maybe I should ring my mum to let her know I'd forgotten my phone. Nah. She'd only have a go and I was sure I'd be home before her anyway. She'd never know.

*

We sat on top of the hill with its green summer grass. The ruined stone priory was to our left, all dramatic and decaying, just crying out for someone to do a painting of it or take a photograph. In front of us was the North Sea, calm and flat, a tanker placed out near the blue glazed horizon to make it look empty and give it depth perspective. And still just the one small puffy white cloud in the blue summer sky. We sat cross-legged, looking out for signs of crowds forming, idly picking up grass and watching it getting carried away in the breeze from left to right. Fluffy was on the far left on the line as we looked out. Her sleeveless fluffy white top swished in the breeze like it was seaweed swaying underwater. Then there was me in my black vest, struggling to control my black, wild woman hair. Then there was Holly in her red vest, then Sarah G-String, controlling the flapping on her bubblewrap jacket.

"When's it going to happen, then?" said Holly.

"Any minute," said Fluffy, tapping her watch and beaming, "any minute."

✢

"And who's coming?" asked Sarah G-String.

"Everybody!"

"Not everybody," said G-String, "not our grans and that!"

"No," said Fluffy with her hands up in exasperation, "just everybody in the know."

"Like you!" said Holly.

"Like me," said Fluffy, looking expectantly round a full 180 degrees, then back again and 180 round the other way.

"So what happens," I said, "if no one turns up?"

Fluffy tapped her watch again.

"Will you look at that sky," said Holly, "only one cloud in it. What a great day – there's no way it's going to rain today."

"Holly!" I shouted and Fluffy joined in.

"So, that's the end of school," said G-String.

"Finally," said Holly.

It *was* our last day of school. For Fluffy it was art college next. For

Maurice Suckling

Holly, university. For Sarah G-String a job in a department store in town. For me, I wanted to travel, do everything, go everywhere, be an explorer, live abroad, invent stuff, discover stuff, be famous or infamous by the time I was 30 – but I'd probably end up just getting a job as a receptionist somewhere. Mum needed help with the house bills.

"We could go get ice creams," said Holly.

"You know," said Fluffy, "even though I'm really excited about all the stuff we're gonna do, a little bit of me knows that the looking forward to it bit is the best bit, and nothing ever gets any better than this. Does it?"

"You mean sitting on a hill?" said Holly.

A sound behind us. A skewer-ended alien probe had drilled through the sky from another universe at warp speed. We all ducked and nearly got sucked into the vortex of G-Force whooshing from it. My body sent my brain chemicals it must have been storing for just such an event. My legs were shaking as I sat cross-legged watching the fighter jet climb back up towards the single white cloud.

*

We said swearwords on reflex like a flock of seagulls till we used them all up.

"Let's go before that happens again," I said.

"Who wants to slide down on bums?" said Holly.

"No way!" said G-String. "I'll do my bum in!"

And that made the rest of us laugh.

"*I will!* I'll do it in!…Stop it! What's wrong with you? Are you all mental cases?"

We were starting to cry with laughter. I keeled over to one side.

"That's it then! I'm walking round."

And G-String walked off on her longcut along the road and my sides hurt.

Me, Fluffy and Holly slid down the hill on our bums, scudding down in our jeans screaming. Holly was loudest, but I was quickest to the bottom. I turned round to see the other two. Holly was second and as she stopped she screamed in a different way – higher, but there was something wrong. Glass in her foot. I took it out. Bright red blood that ran down her foot like ink.

"Can you walk on it?"

"Yeah," she said, "it's ok as long as I don't run."

We started making our way onto the sand of the beach towards Sarah G-String.

"Wow, look at that," said Fluffy.

She was looking upwards. There were a hundred blue thought bubbles drifting high into the sky. Each one exactly the shape and colour of a thought, some bumping into each other, others drifting off to get lost or to find somewhere never been before, and all of them so light they just got higher and higher, until it seemed they were being eaten by the sun.

*

"I love balloons," said Holly as we stared at them crook-necked on auto-pilot.

Then we bumped into some people. Three boys with surfboards under their arms, licking ice creams and looking up at the balloons. We all apologised.

"Well hello girls," said the tallest with black hair – the leader.

"Hello boys," said Holly.

"You having fun?" said their leader.

"We were," said Holly.

"We're all about fun, girls," said the shortest with blue shorts. They all had bare tanned tops and tattoos on the side of their shoulders.

"We *were* having fun," said Holly, sneaking a look at their ice creams, "but then we grew weak from hunger and realised we needed ice cream."

"There's a van on the other hill," said the leader, pointing over the other side of the beach.

"But we're too weak," said Holly. "Perhaps if you bought us an ice cream we'd have enough energy to get there."

"And what do you do when you've got energy?" asked the shortest one.

"Are you coming onto me, Mr Surfer Boy?"

"You fancy a ride on my long hard board, shoeless girl?"

Suddenly Holly nudged the ice creams into their faces with quick magician's hands: one, two, three, then legged it. Me and Fluffy ran after her as she headed off across the beach. We had a head start on the boys as I heard them slice their surfboards into the sand like fins. The sand was so deep it was hard to run, my feet were sinking past my ankles. Then a sand octopus with tentacles the size of elephant trunks lunged up from the depths of its lair, lashed round my right foot and dragged me down into the grainy caverns of its suffocating world. I fought the tentacles and swung my arms wildly, managing to break free to the surface to see Holly falling down in the sand, before the monster dragged me back down, and down again.

*

"Did the sand trip you up?" said their leader, peering over me.

Holly had fallen over with her bad foot and with the two of us down Fluffy stopped running and came back for us. Their leader picked me up and carried me laughing towards where Fluffy and Holly were sitting cross-legged in the sand. They were waving to Sarah G-String who'd spotted us and was just making her way across the beach.

"We're their hostages," explained Holly to her when she asked what we were doing and who the boys were.

"New ice creams to get your friends back," said the leader, "two of you can go, and two stay here."

"Do you have girlfriends?" asked Sarah G-String sternly.

"No, we don't," said the other one who'd not spoken before. He had a silver dolphin on the end of his necklace.

I saw Fluffy blush.

Me and Sarah G-String were the designated ice cream getterers and set off towards the van on top of the hill the far side of where we'd come from. There was a rash of people spread all over the place, beach towels, sunhats, sunglasses, deckchairs, cool-boxes, hampers, people in the sea, li-los and kids with inflatable animals and armbands, kids running, kids getting towelled down, minor dramas with fingers and toes, grown ups lying down with eyes closed, cans of pop opening, seagulls squawking, the smell of salt water.

In the long queue for the van were two girls in bikinis about our age in front of us with beads in their hair. They both had beach-lovers' tans.

"You seen them yet?" said blue bikini.

"Not yet. You think they know we're here?" said green bikini.

There were eight people in front of us, including the girls. It was an old style van with a large stuck-on ice cream sculpture in chipped paint on the front. The van was chugging with the cooler motor in that way you take for granted until it stops, and then you realise how loud it was. It stopped.

"Ohoh," said blue bikini, "I think I just saw them."

"Really? You sure it's them?"

"Go check."

Green bikini stepped out of the queue and stood at the edge of the wall overlooking the beach. Neither of these girls had a ripple of cellulite.

"She'll get leathery skin," said Sarah G-String under her breath, looking at her too.

"Yeah, you're right," she said, rushing back in front of us in the queue. "It's them; they're the only guys on the beach with surfboards."

*

"No ice creams no freedom," said their leader, with his white teeth.

"Oh, there are gonna be ice creams, they just ran out for a bit," I said.

"They're still serving," said the short one on tiptoes looking up to the van on the hill.

"Just drinks," said G-String. "We'll go back in a bit and get them – and none of us are going anywhere 'til then."

"Ok," said their leader, "so if we went and caught a few waves you might still be here?"

"Of course," I said, trying to make my eyebrows go high and rounded.

*

We watched them head towards the shore and waved. We waited till they were in the water then we ran through the clusters of people. Two sunbather groups away we found three towels and three piles of clothes. The three of us looked at each other. Then we picked up a pile each then turned and ran to the sea.

11

"Hey!" we shouted.

We got their attention out on their boards in the mid-distance.

"Hey!" they shouted back.

"These your clothes?" shouted out Holly.

We hoyed their clothes into the sea, turned and legged it.

"How-Way!" Their leader was the loudest. The sand was deep, like quicksand again. It was like running in a dream. You try but you don't really get anywhere. Your legs can't seem to grip on anything so it makes your arms go even faster.

When we turned round the boys were getting near the shore, rescuing their clothes. We tried to keep running through the sand and they started running towards us again.

"Split up!" shouted Fluffy.

So she went left and I went right, and G-String and Holly went straight on. I ducked round the corner of the sailing club hut and caught my breath. I watched as the boys started to go after Fluffy, then changed their mind and went after Holly and G-String.

Then they stopped and gave up. They were too far behind.

I caught my breath for a bit where I was and felt all hot and sweaty. I sneaked round the side of the club hut and couldn't see the boys.

I went to the edge of the beach and cupped a double-hander of water and splashed it over my oven-face, another one on my neck. It trickled down my back the way I imagine the roots of an ice tree would grow.

Then I looked up, and there she was, floating on a giraffe patterned li-lo wearing a black swimsuit and a pair of baby pink star-framed sunnies.

"Like total hi," she said, reclined, bobbing up and down, doing her American teenager voice – her favourite accent of the moment.

"Grannie! What are you doing here?" She lived on her own, was thirty miles from home, couldn't drive and knew no one, apart from my mum, who had a car.

"I'm, like, totally on a li-lo in the North Sea," and she kicked her feet off the end of the li-lo and paddled with her hands on either side, pushing herself a little further out away from the shore.

"Grannie! Come back! And stop doing that voice, it drives me mental! Where's mum?" I couldn't see her. "What are you doing here?"

"I opened the fridge door and that teleported me here by accident – I think it was the milk what did it – or the stilton – that was months out of date."

"Grannie!"

"I mean, I hi-jacked the ice cream van and drove it here to come paddling – I couldn't turn the siren off so the kids ran after me – kids, run fast these days, don't they…I mean, I died, then snuck all the way back to try and bump into you here."

"Grannie!!"

*

Back at the car Grannie didn't have any other clothes apart from her black swimsuit and flip-flops, so she put my long grey cardigan round her shoulders. We deflated her giraffe li-lo and put it in the boot. I was just punching my mum's work number into G-String's phone when Grannie asked me not to.

"Please dear, don't worry about that nonsense," she said. "It'll just cause trouble. You know what your mum's like."

"So are you going to tell me what you're doing here alone?" I asked, settling her into the front passenger seat.

"Oh yes, dear," she said, "but not yet." Then she put her star framed sunnies over her eyes.

I got Fluffy to go to my Grannie's first and to wait while I took her and her giraffe li-lo inside. She didn't have her keys on her, but I had a set on my key-ring. Once the door was closed I got a towel from the downstairs bathroom and wrapped it round her.

"Would you like to tell me how you got to the beach, Grannie? I won't tell mum, if you don't want me to." I dried her hair.

"I think I'd like to go to bed, sweetheart," she said. "I'm not feeling at my best."

"Ok, let's get you into bed, then."

She looked pale and her forehead was a little warm, but she got up the stairs without much help and managed to undress and re-dress herself in her best nightie – the one with all the little lace patterns on the trim and a flower like a dandelion on the bust. I drew the curtains back, put her bedside table lamp on, took her pink sunnies off and put them next to it, then asked if she'd like a cup of tea.

Maurice Suckling

She wanted me to sit on the bed, and took my hand.
"Are you sure, Grannie? It's no bother."
"No thank you dear. I just wanted to see you."
I stroked her hand with my thumb.

*

When Fluffy dropped me home mum's car was on the street outside.
The girl's gave me their *best of lucks* and I said I'd better go in. She was
sitting at the kitchen table, a cup of tea in front of her, and my phone
next to it.
"Hello Mum," I said, trying to sound nonchalant.
She hit me with one of her steel looks and said nothing. I made a
snap decision to tell her.
"Mum, I need to tell you something about Grannie."
She stood up. "I've been trying to call you all day, Elaine." It felt
uncalled for to use my name and unnecessarily mean. She picked up my
phone with one hand and waggled it. "But I've not been able to, have I?
How many times do I have to tell you?" She shook her head and said,
"Grannie died in the morning."

*

Today, two years after that happened, I took the lift. I work in a local
office as a receptionist. On the second floor my Grannie got on, kissed
me on the cheek, handed me an envelope, gave me a hug, and got out
on the third floor. There was no one else in the lift.
I spent the day making mistakes and mixing up callers, wondering
why no words had come out of my mouth, why my legs hadn't moved,
why I hadn't tried to chase after her and speak to her. I went down to
the third floor every break but no one was there. It was still empty,
waiting for a new company to move in.
I waited till I got home to open the envelope. A photograph.
It was taken back on my 18th birthday. Me, Fluffy, Holly and Sarah
G-String had gone swimming in the afternoon and my Grannie had
come with us. I didn't know she had a camera with her. She must have
snapped as the four of us leapt off the side of the pool. She caught us
high up in mid air, with nothing else in shot except us and the white wall
of the pool behind; all of us smiling so big it looks like our faces will
burst.

Identity Renting

Rumours were, Nyoko, the new girl was happy. I'd been at the store over a year and seen all sorts, I can tell you. Nyoko, small, dark bobbed hair with dyed pink streaks, pierced lower lip (silver stud), black Doc Martens, black dress, one white arm with a cheap digital watch with a green LED light, her other white arm full of silver bracelets, had been there a week. She smiled and looked relaxed and liked being helpful when people wanted to rent DVDs. I knew she wouldn't be here long. She'd move on and do something else. This was just a stepping stone for her.

At the start of the second week, when our shifts overlapped, I asked her if the rumours were true. 'Shucks, Zander, I guess they are,' she said, sounding evasive, which I interpreted as encouraging. I went back to my flat a few streets away and played computer games. I shot my way through an underground bunker, only to be killed right near the end in almost exactly the same spot over and over again. I went to bed late, annoyed with the game. It was a waste of time.

By the next morning I had formulated a plan. I would spy to see what movies Nyoko took home to watch; see if watching them would make me happy like her. This was much the same plan as I had formulated six months ago, when it seemed that Crispin was happy. In the week I began the experiment he watched *The Odd Couple*, *Goldfinger*, *War of the Worlds*, *Kramer versus Kramer*, then drank a bottle of vodka and half a tub of pain-killers, filled the bath, left a suicide note, was discovered by neighbours complaining about the leaking water, and never came back to work.

For the next ten days Nyoko watched:

i) Midnight Cowboy
ii) Benny and Joon
iii) Secretary
iv) This Is Spinal Tap
v) Strangers on a Train
vi) Magnolia
vii) The Machinist
viii) Ghandi
ix) 9 to 5
x) Solaris - remake

Each day she returned the DVD from the previous night, and I took it to my flat and watched it.

I felt just the same as ever. It wasn't working.

I had the weekend off. I spoke to my flatmates Jurgen and Svetlana in the pub. I told them about my plan. We had a table outside. It was sticky with spilt beer and there were empty folded crisp packet triangles stuffed between its slats.

Jurgen said that I shouldn't try to be someone else. He said I should just be myself. I looked across incredulously at Svetlana who, unbelievably, agreed with him.

Jurgen wouldn't leave it be and started listing things I had to look forward to. I'd had just about enough of him by now and punched him full on the mouth, making him spill his drink. As I walked away, telling both of them I was not sorry at all, I realised that Jurgen had inadvertently stumbled onto something. I had been holding back. To be like Nyoko I would need to have Nyoko's friends. I had no doubt they were brilliant and funny and smart and kind and thoughtful and excellent cooks and not leave bits of marmalade in the butter. It was my friends who were holding me back. I realised now, in a sequence of flashbacks recounting many years of looks between them I hadn't understood at the time, remembering half-heard words passed between them that I could now, finally, fill in the blanks for, this had always been their intention.

I decided to ramp up my plan. I wouldn't just watch the same DVDs as Nyoko. I wouldn't just have the same friends as her. I would be as much like her as I could.

On the Monday Nyoko watched *Austin Powers: Goldmember*. Luckily we had two copies in the store and I watched it the same night.

Tuesday I overheard Nyoko saying the name of the pub she was meeting her friends at. I went on my own, saw her at a table and she beckoned me over. I said I was supposed to be meeting my friends, but they hadn't turned up. She introduced me to her flatmates, Klaus and Tatyana. They were very funny and interesting and I made them laugh lots. Nyoko used the phrase 'sting in the tail'. I was concentrating on the way her lips curled as she said it so I missed the context.

Wednesday I started speaking like Nyoko.

"Is *Memento* still out, Zander?" My boss, Tariq, asked.

"Shucks, Tariq, guess I'll just check. Shucks, guess it is. Shucks, how about that?"

"What's with this shucks shit all of a sudden?"

"It's the sting in the tail."

I grinned.

Tariq looked at me funny.

Thursday was special. I came to work in a black dress with bobbed black hair with pink streaks in it. The hairdresser had needed constant reassurance. I tipped her well for the life and bounce she was finally able to give me. I wore a cheap digital watch with a green LED light on one arm and a curtain rail of silver bracelets I'd bought from the market on the other. I also wore my new lip stud. I'd done it myself with a needle and an ice cube. It hurt. I used talcum powder to cover up the red rash round it. Nyoko was back at work. She said 'what the fuck?' and screwed her face up on one side. I said 'what the fuck?' with exactly the same tone and screwed my face up just the same as she had. I did everything and said everything she did, only a few seconds after her. When she told me to fuck off I stood in exactly the same pose and told her to fuck off. When I said it she left. I decided I ought to stay to the end of my shift. For the last hour I insisted all the customers call me Nyoko or I wouldn't let them rent anything.

Friday I was barely through the door when Tariq said, "Zander, I need to see you." I refused to acknowledge him till he referred to me correctly. He was stubborn and refused at first, but eventually saw I

Maurice Suckling

would out-patience him. (Nyoko is *always* patient with everyone.)

It was as I feared. Tariq said I either needed to sort myself out or I would have to think about finding somewhere else to work. He told me to take the rest of the day off.

I didn't want to think about finding anywhere else to work, not yet. This video store had probably been the best place I'd worked, ever, and I wasn't ready to start looking for somewhere else just yet. This was a blow. I was left to weigh my thoughts on the sex change and the name change application I had been planning.

Unable to settle in my flat I found myself wandering out in the night to where I knew Nyoko lived. I'd found her address earlier in the week, before someone locked the drawer in the office where the book was kept. I didn't need to double-check it, I already knew for sure what it was and I'd written it over the walls in my bedroom in permanent marker. I made a slip at one point when Jurgen and Svetlana's banging on my door had got suddenly louder, but I managed to cover up the mistake by turning the dot on the 'i' in her address into a halo. I'd only gone back to find the book so I could look at her handwriting again. I was finding her 'g' and 'y' tails hard to replicate.

The door to her garden was open. I walked through and found a place under a bush where I could look up into her bedroom – her light on and curtain open. She sat at a desk writing something, looking up from time to time, while I turned my thoughts over and over, wondering what, if Nyoko were me, she would do next.

I half-woke from half-sleep in the mist-filled not-morning feeling achy and sore, like I'd been leaning against a hard wet sponge all night with my eyes closed. The night was struggling unconvincingly to flip itself inside out and turn into the day. And that's when it happened.

Between 5.17am and 5.24am I felt it. I timed it on my cheap digital watch, using the green LED.

There I was, thinking about Nyoko's day ahead, about her waking up, her morning wee, her sleep-fugged dreams still musty round her, the clothes she'd wear, the people she'd speak to, the things she'd see, the food she'd eat, the movie she'd watch at work today – *The Guru*, I guessed, and it was there. Inside me. Not whizzing round me. But moving slowly in my body like a giant wave seen from the distance, and at the same time I was inside it. And safe. Flying above it, but somehow it was tugging me along, or I was tugging it along with me. Happiness. Between 5.17 am and 5.24 am.

I made my way back to my flat. I had a shower. There was no hot water. My towel was still in the washing machine. There was no milk left in the fridge.

Things You Can See

I went to Japan and took the best photo ever. That's what my friend Laura at art college said.

"Fluffy, that's the best photo ever." I got the name Fluffy at school coz of the fluffy blue coat I used to have, and the boots and steering wheel, and other stuff. I still had the jacket and the name stuck through art college.

My tutor liked it too. He said he liked the colour of the cherry blossoms and wondered how I'd thought of composing the picture the way I had with the branches of the trees interlacing like DNA.

He said the only other photo he'd ever seen anywhere near this good was by a girl at the same college two years before.

"Did she take it with her?" I asked.

"No," he said, "it got fire alarmed."

Fire alarming was a renowned practice at college. Someone would trigger the alarm, people would file out the building and when they came back in they'd find artwork taken off the walls. It was college, so people stole things they wanted, and it was art college so they wanted art.

The truth was I knew the picture could have been much better. I knew what Laura and my tutor and all the other people who liked it saw in it. But I knew it was missing something vital. I just wasn't sure what.

When you take a photo you're freezing an image. A cherry blossom in a photo is a representation of a cherry blossom, not the thing itself. Visual art is an abstraction. An image is an idea with its clothes on. An image keeps you on this side of the paper and stops you seeing anything on the other side of it. What was bothering me was how to really get at the thing itself, how to take its clothes off and see the idea, how to see something the other side of the paper.

Maurice Suckling

I started mucking about with photography techniques, different exposure times, trying to find a way of getting at what I was after. People kept looking over my shoulder to see what I was doing. Pretty soon it seemed everyone in my year knew what I was working on. Even people in the year above and the year below knew me as the cherry blossom girl. Everyone was whispering about how I was going to win the college prize that year.

I should have been more careful. My negatives were stolen. They were fire alarmed. I thought they'd be safe in my drawer. It could have been anyone. I heard people whispering in the corridors about how everyone with brains worked in digital these days.

I was devastated. I didn't go into college for a week. But then, I thought, I still have my prints. I picked up where my experiments had left off. I worked hard.

I was amazed when I won the college art prize for my submission. I was polite, but I knew I'd failed. I still couldn't get at the thing itself. I still was only showing a representation of the cherry blossom, only showing what people wanted it to look like, what they expected it to be like. I still wasn't getting at the idea behind the thing. The idea still had its clothes on.

Later that afternoon the fire alarm went. I rushed to the main hall, against the flow of people, because I was sure someone was trying to steal my prize winning print. I ran down the corridor and bumped my head. I bumped it very hard. I didn't wake up for three days.

I was taken to hospital, but I don't remember any of that. All I remember is, when they let me out, I was sitting in my mum's car on our way back home, looking out of the window. We pulled up at traffic lights and there was a big white wall to my left. As I daydreamed I could see my print on that wall – the cherry blossoms as pink as the first day of the first spring, the branches interlacing like DNA. There it was, the way you can see the light from a bulb after you've looked away. Wherever you look, there it is. And then, behind the print, as simple as blinking again, I could see the negatives and as I just kept on looking and blinking slowly to refresh the view, there was the idea. The thing itself, the idea of cherry blossom without its clothes on. It hurt to look at it for too long.

I suppose Dave and Naomi are off on holiday again, somewhere hot,

I had to wipe the sleep away from my eyes the next morning. Only it wasn't sleep. It was layers and layers of the pinkest, newest cherry blossoms you ever did see.

I stored them carefully in a tin box under my bed. The box has a lock on it.

I have drawn up a list of everything I plan to see next.

THE AMAZING ADVENTURES OF NO ONE IN PARTICULAR

Episode 1

Usually I would be sitting at my desk.

But I wasn't.

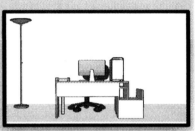

I looked at my watch. It was 10:10 and 10 seconds.

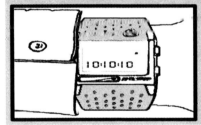

By now I'd be slipping from the *late* to the *not coming in* category in their minds.

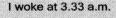

Last week I was 33.

I woke at 3.33 a.m.

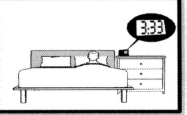

I thought WOW!

I thought, a tiny thought, of ringing my friends to tell them.

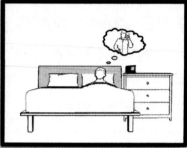

But by then it would be 3.34 a.m.

Today, instead of being at my desk...

...I was looking out of a train window.

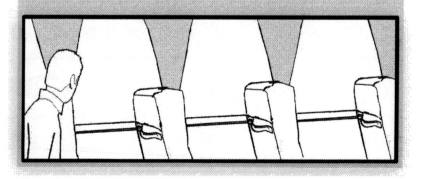

I saw fields...

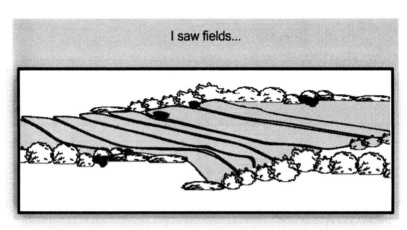

...hills...

...and trees.

I thought 'Wow, how green everything is'.

27

On this morning I woke at 7:17.

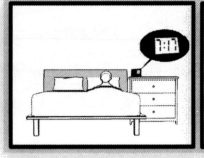

I didn't think anything in particular.

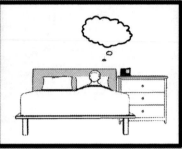

But then I pictured me at work right through the day.

And the day just didn't seem to need me...

...to actually be there.

So I walked to the station.

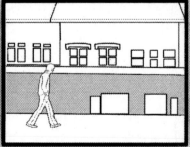

Part Two

A New Kitchen Is A Way To A New Life

The Photo

Page 27 of the MFI kitchen catalogue; modern styling, cream unit doors with ultra thin long chrome handles, dark teak floors and kitchen table. Far left of the frame, in the foreground, a small tanned contented boy in muted blue sits at the table pouring milk from a white jug into his white bowl. Centre-frame, towards the back, in white with long black hair, the mum smiles contently at the work-surface by the chrome sink, chopping fresh bright vegetables on a thick wooden board. To her right, mid ground and perfectly balancing the triptych, in greys at the coffee plunger, the handsome dark-haired dad beams a white-toothed grin diagonally across the frame back to the boy. Perfect harmony.

Beginning

It was that photo that did it for me. It could have been one of any number. But it was that one. I found it in the MFI brochure we'd picked up when we were in a store the week earlier and I'd finally got round to looking at it lying on the lounge sofa on the Sunday afternoon. We were listening to the *Flaming Lips* CD about the robot.

"What?" said Dave, my boyfriend, from the comfy chair. "Hailey! What is it? You've been looking at the same page for the last ten minutes."

I musta been doing his nut. I never got a full 'Hailey' unless I was doing his nut.

I flung it over to him.

He pulled a face.

"There you go. Page 27. You tell me."

He looked at me. Found the page. Looked at the photo. Then looked back at me.

"You like it?"

"What?"

"This is the one you want?" he said.

"Dave you're such a twat!"

He pulled a face.

"You don't like it?"

"Don't say it like that, like you're my dad. What do you think?"

"I think…"

"You'll get it wrong, Dave. It's not about the kitchen, it's about what I'm turning into; what we're both turning into."

"Which is?" said Dave, sounding like my dad.

"People who buy kitchens."

"You agreed when we moved in we had to…"

"I'm not talking about that. I'm talking about the staged perfection, the way you're made to feel like you have to try and have this unattainable life where you too can have a husband who grins while he percolates fresh coffee in his bare feet, and a kid who pours himself fresh cold milk from a perfect white jug into his perfect white bowl as he sits at the table happy and clean in his new clothes and you slice food happily with your perfect skin between glasses of mineral water in new bottles on your vast spotless marble surfaces in your large uncluttered kitchen."

"Wo!" he said, holding his hands up, like I was now a horse. "What's wrong with people aiming for something like that? They have to aim for something. It's not like it's dangerous or anything."

"Of course it's fucking dangerous." Dave was really starting to piss me off now.

"You're still pissed off my phone is better than yours aren't you?"

I stormed out.

He came upstairs fifteen minutes later with a cup of tea. I managed to shut down the computer before he found me searching the internet for a newer, smaller mobile than his with more up to date features.

Middle

Two weekends later we were in the same store, walking around, looking at bathrooms. We'd decided to make a start there, and work our way up to the kitchen decision over the next few weeks. In the Aegean display Dave bumped into his ex-girlfriend, Naomi. Her tan was topped up as usual, which means she will get leather skin at this rate. I got bored of standing around looking happy to see her with my face stuck in grin mode, so I left them to it and said I'd be in the kitchens.

Maybe I already knew where I was going to end up. If I did I didn't let onto me until I'd looked through a Rimini kitchen, a Woodbridge one, a Conway and a Wessex Pine. I didn't even know for sure if they had the kitchen from the photo in the store. But when I was standing in the Chatsworth display I saw it and I realised I'd been looking for it all along.

The display was smaller than the one in the photo, and was missing some of its more stylish kitchen accessories, and the models, of course. I wiped the palm of my hand over its almost frictionless clean cold surface. I moved the head of the tap up, and moved it down. I drummed my fingers on the bottom of the aluminium sink. I opened doors. I closed them. I opened two at once, and closed them. I looked at storage space inside the units. I let this kitchen know I was not taken in. I let it know I knew it was just a kitchen.

More Middle

Six weeks later I hadn't seen much of Dave, he'd been working late. We'd made no progress with either the bathroom or the kitchen.

I'd been collecting more brochures and visiting more stores in that time. I had a collection of eighteen brochures from all the stores in a forty mile radius.

Dave said I was becoming obsessive, and I sensed a distance growing between us.

End

When Dave walked out on me – he was going back to Naomi – we still hadn't done any work to the house. We sold it in pretty much the exact state we'd bought it in.

Maurice Suckling

knowing her skin and his imagination.

I used to have a small bedsit in the soon to be done up railway station end of town. Lunchtimes, evenings and weekends I used to spend as much time as possible in home improvement stores. Then I started going in the mornings too and soon stopped going to work at all. A few months after that I lost my bedsit.

I now spend all my time walking round the kitchen displays of various local stores imagining my life in each kitchen. I open doors, decide where the appliances ought to be, stand at the sink and at surfaces, and sit at tables and breakfast bars. The people who work there come and ask if they can help, which is nice, but I always say 'I'm fine, thank you', because they're not supposed to be in there too or it ruins it for me, and I think they know it from the way they look so uncomfortable. In quite a few stores now they've got to know me and they mostly let me be until they have to close the store and I thank them very much and say 'I'll see you tomorrow' and wave them goodnight.

In recent weeks I swear, if I close my eyes, I am even starting to see myself as I start to cut through the freshest of fresh bread on a thick wooden chopping board, the avocadoes next to me wonderfully ripe, the coffee percolating as my man, in his bare feet, grins in an unfathomably handsome way at our perfectly behaved small boy, and there's not a single crack in any of the porcelain, or a single smear on any of the chrome fittings, handles or cappuccino cups.

Nowhere
And Other Destinations You Can Enjoy

1

"Markmark's rightright! What's the worst that could happen?" said Cab, from the back of our rented three door swamp green Vauxhall Corsa. I turned round to see him semi-lit by the motorway's Lucozade midnight light, sitting forward with his eyes wide and his palms out.

"We all die of bad yellow poison and fall in a vat of bland watery soup…" said Hassan, out of the dark next to Cab. "…And get eaten by crocodiles…dressed as Westlife doing a…oover of…*Smells Like Teen Spirit.*"

"No, that's not the worst! A long way from it!" said Wood, who was driving.

"How could that be a lot worse, Wood?" I said, because right then I had a very vivid picture of all the crocodiles in white jumpers and trousers, doing the song all ballad-stylie and looking all video-sad to camera.

Wood looked into her central mirror as she flicked the indicator, then pulled out and overtook the people carrier in front.

"There could be sprouts in the soup," she said.

"Errr," said Hassan, like he meant it.

So, there not being any kind of reply to my question that amounted to much, we all went back easily enough to pretending I'd never asked it and sank back into as-you-were dispositions.

The cars we passed at night all seemed lost but too on their own to ask for directions, like they'd just have to keep going till it got day, and only then could they work out where they were and how far they'd gone.

As we passed the last sign, at the last moment before it would be dangerous, Cab let out a: 'can we stop, pleeeeeeeeaaaase'. Wood looked in her mirror, flicked her indicator and a few seconds later she dipped into the escape lane and started slowing down, like she was expecting it.

Wood parked near the entrance, almost a whole carpark to choose from. We started to unfold legs and do stretches as Hassan said he thought we should take our stuff in with us, because he had a feeling the car was going to be broken into.

"What all of it?" said Cab, moving round to the open boot, where you could make out the bulk of the 'it' he meant.

"No, just the stuff you don't want nicked," said Hassan, like this was obvious, and picked up his own bag and handed Wood's bag to her.

"You're not taking your sleeping bag, then?" says Cab.

"Nah, they can have that," said Hassan, handing me and Cab our bags.

I looked at Wood.

"Come on then," she said, and we headed inside, through concrete and glass and large orange reminders everywhere about the astonishingly good value of a full breakfast, plus tea or coffee, in the café.

"Got a sort of post-Apocalypse, vibe, don't it," said Hassan, as we failed to see anyone else around another corner.

"Yep," said Wood, "all function and no one to functionise it."

"There's us," Cab pointed out.

"We don't count," said Hassan, like this was even more obvious than the previous obvious thing.

The trick with the café was to get in and make some selections, pay and eat, before your appetite twigged what you were up to. Hassan was too slow and ended up trying to put a banana out of its misery, but even gave up on that after a few small bites. Mostly he drank coffee; three cups. He likes coffee. I'd already managed to eat the pasta dish, and started to pick at the bread roll before I realised it didn't taste very nice.

"It *will* be snowing, right?" said Hassan, dancing his banana skin round his tray, like a sea thingie.

"Yeah," I said, "loads, be impossible to get through, there'll be tailbacks of snow-ploughs all trying to get to work on time."

"Excellent," said Hassan, jumping his banana slow motion style over onto my tray.

"And people skiing and wearing tennis racket shoes...," said Wood, "...oh, and a snow creature with white fur and enormous feet, the size of...well, big feet...people skiing away from the snow creature so they don't get eaten – I guess the people with the tennis racket shoes will get eaten coz they're slower."

"That's a lot of snow," said Cab.

"I guess there's a lot of snow out there, and it's all got to go somewhere," said Hassan, nodding sort of to himself, sort of not.

"Dammit, you're right," said Wood, "and more to the point, it's got to go *there*. Why would it want to go anywhere else?"

The new year just after we all left university, Cab said, "Why don't we rent a cottage, and go and.........do.........stuff." So we did. To the four of us at the time it was pretty far north, and we'd all hoped it was going to snow. It didn't. I remember it as this odd little cliff-edge time. We drank cheap wine that made our lips and tongues purpley-red and talked rubbish about stuff we were gonna do, and all that nonsense. Then we went off and did our lives, or made a start at them at any rate. We set a ten year timer for the reunion. The original plan was to have a few nights there. But Hassan now had to work and it got knocked back to one night. After the four hours we'd just spent in the traffic jam heading north it was now going to be even less than a night.

Cab has settled into a cash and carry lifestyle. He works for a bit, mostly bars and outdoors equipment shops, then he packs his rucksack and he's off again. Africa, Asia, India, Indonesia. South America next. His skin's got that brown weathered look, and he's lost almost any sense of squeamishness about anything. He also doesn't seem to feel the cold anymore. Mostly he seems to wear one of his traveller's t-shirts from somewhere in the world, and I've even seen him wearing sandals here in October. But he still has an enthusiasm that's good to be around, like one of the night time ocean-side beach fires he'll tell you about from time to time. He usually operates on a three-monthly cycle, but he came back specially for this.

Wood is an actress. Beautiful and small and smart and struggling.

She gets small parts here and there, always about to be in something that's going to work out, always working hard in shows that aren't going anywhere. Ever since I can remember she was going to be an actress. She's the only one of us who ever had any idea of what to do. Her real name is Holly – so the Wood bit came along at university, stuck, and never went away.

There's me – Mark, or Markmark as they call me, because of the other Marks in our school. I went on a trip to Africa with Cab after university, then I did not very much for a bit, jobs here and there, manual work mostly on short term contracts, then thought I'd better have a thing to do, so went on a TEFL course. I've been to Spain a couple of times to teach, and Portugal once. I've been here the last couple of summers. It doesn't really seem like a permanent thing to do, and I'm wondering if maybe it's time to do something else. But if I think about it for too long the 'like what's?' start and they take a while to go again. If you put your mind to ignoring enough it can work wonders.

Hassan started a PhD in history. He gave up after a year and a half. He started a graduate training scheme for a supermarket chain, and now he's an assistant manager of a 24 hour store. He still lives at home, like Cab and Wood, though Wood used to live with her boyfriend till that went wrong. Hassan works nights whenever he can coz he likes having as much of the rest of his time to think. He says he doesn't think about anything in particular, just whatever his mind digs up from day to day. But I think he thinks about the girl he nearly married more than anything else. This is because he never mentions her at all.

When we got back to the car we could see one of the windows had been smashed, reflecting off the electric light like scattered diced-up amber.

"What did they take?" said Wood, all calm and taking charge. Turned out, they'd taken nothing, not even the sleeping bag Hassan said they could have. Cab ripped off the back of the map and taped it up over the broken window – the one on his side at the back. We had another ninety miles to drive like this, and we should already have been there.

Cab must have been cold. He put a jumper on. Over the sound of the wind pushing through the cardboard he told us about the time in Asia when he was so cold he put on all the clothes that he had, then got in his sleeping bag, then got inside his rucksack.

There was no snow as we got closer. No sign of any snow as we pulled into the carpark of the cottage. There was, however, a thick syrup of nostalgia to pull through.

"Remember that place?" I said. It was a white house by the side of the road, old and cottagey with a big bare tree either side of it.

"Yes," said Wood, scarcely glancing at it, as she kept her eyes to the headlights in the dark of the road.

"Where's that then?" said Cab, though we'd passed it already. "That's where Wood was going to live," I reminded him.

"Maybe a parallel Wood who did different things is already there – which would be handy, we could pop in and say hi and..."

"Be given coffee?" suggested Wood.

"How did you know?" said Hassan.

"Because she's her, so she knows what she'd offer you," I pointed out.

"I like coffee," said Hassan, as if this was a new and interesting Hassan fact.

2

The place was pretty much how we all remembered it. It had been decorated. We all remembered it as blue, though not as blue. The stainless steel sink in the kitchen was just the same. Wood pointed out the dent we made. When you wash and dry and put away in teams you must never throw le creuset pans unless people are looking.

There were three bedrooms. One for Wood, and one for Cab, since he wasn't so used to proper beds, and one for me and Hassan. The bedrooms were just how we remembered them. Middle class, middle age woman, dolls house fixation largely ignored by husband sorta style. We collected together all the rag dolls with their Victorian dresses and put them in the airing cupboard, in case we woke up in the middle of the night and barked in terror at the ghouls on the windowsills.

We had a couple of beers in the lounge – red swirly what kind of shape is that? – patterned carpet, with a who-would-design-that-on-purpose-style sofa and suite. Cab, though, had one and a bit beers, because he spilt most of his second one on the carpet. We tried clearing it up with washing up liquid. But it made so much foam it took ages to get it out. We moved the coffee table over it instead.

"Markmark," you're up, said Wood, slumped in the biggest armchair, which made her look tiny.

Hassan lit the candles he bought specially. With the room light off we were left with a patchy red-yellow underglow.

Wood said she hoped we didn't set the house on fire.

Everyone told her off for jinxing.

"My story's about Rory," I began, "and Rory passed some important exams." I paused so everyone would know just how important these exams really were.

"Rory was in a class of thirty, and only the best ten from each year passed, and Rory was in that top ten. Now, this is a big deal for him and everyone else who's passed because it means he now has access to the top floor of The Tower. The Tower is a dominating hundred-floor glass block overlooking the river, right at the heart of the city where he lives."

"What's the city called?" asked Hassan.

"It's called...Success City, in the Land of Success. The whole city, the whole land is founded on the drive and desire people have to get into this one hundred meter square room. It's everything this city is about, everything all ten million of its inhabitants dream about, everything the whole land is about. This one room, and the aspiration of people to get into it is the only thing people care about."

"So it's important?" said Hassan.

"So it's important." I paused. "Ok, the top floor of The Tower is renowned for its opulence and luxury. There are tales of revolving restaurant floors, of lush interiors and a surround-sound mini cinema. Tales are told of unimaginable wonders and splendour, and of unfathomable sensations.

"Now, like the other nine students from his year, Rory is given a swipe card and a password to the top floor. But when Rory goes up to the floor for the first time, swipes his card and enters the password, the tiny red light in the security box stays red and he can't get in. He takes the lift down to the basement to speak to security. He checks the password, but he had it right. They check the swipe card, and find no fault with it.

"'Maybe you could come up and help, then,' says Rory, 'because I don't understand why it's doing that.'

"The security guard shakes his head from side to side, 'na na na na na na na'.

"He looks over the top of his newspaper, the *Daily Mail*, and shakes his head some more.

"'Can't leave here. Rules.'

"Rory – a trier – takes the lift back up to the top floor and tries again. He swipes the card and enters the password. The tiny red security light stays red – doesn't even blip. Just then Mala, from his year group, opens the door, stepping out of the interior of the room. The sound of voices laughing and screaming with excitement and giggling over music all tumble out, before the door closes on them and she steps clear. She notices Rory and blushes a 'hi'.

"He 'hi's her back, going a little red himself. It's the romance everyone in their year thought was going to happen but never did. Mala steps towards the lift and presses the button to call it.

"'Hey, Mala,' he says before he can stop himself. 'Can you get in there alright?' His forefinger points lamely at the closed door.

"'Um, sure,' she says in a neutral, sort of puzzled tone, tossing her long straight blonde hair back behind her tiny attractive ears.

"'Oh, right,' he says, then takes a step towards her and speaks softer.

"'So what's it like?' She ducks her head a little closer towards his and speaks soft as well.

"'Bit disappointing, really.' Then the lift doors open with a bing and she steps in.

"'Bye,' she says.

"'Bye,' he says and the lift doors close."

3

The heating packed in. We spent half an hour trying to fix it, reading the instructions in the booklet we found on top of the boiler. We couldn't fix it. We took the blankets off our beds and wrapped ourselves up in them. I knocked over my third beer with the tail of my blanket. We moved the sofa to help cover it up.

It was Wood's story next.

"This is about Fran, who's an actress, one of those pretty home-county type girls," she said, in the almost not-light of the candles. One of them was already starting to putter.

"Fran is pretty, but not sleazy enough to really get noticed. She's struggling and still looking for the big break, when she gets a rare call from her agent, who she's been thinking of ditching, for, well, about...four years.

"'Jan!' Drawls the agent in her luvvie voice, 'it's me, Arabella'.

"'Fran,' corrects Fran politely, with a hint of impatience that shocks her she let slip.

"'Yes dear, I have an audition for you – super, perfect for you, have you ever been a cowgirl before?'

"'No...does that matter?'

"'It's perfect for you. You do do guns, don't you?'

"'How do you mean?'

"'You know, hats and guns, super, I'll send details soon as. Mwah!'

"And, for once, she does phone back with the details. So, the next day, Fran turns up, clutching a scrap of paper in her hand with the address on it, and gingerly knocks on the door.

"'Hello, I'm...'

"And she is hugged and dragged inside by a large group of fawning busying people.

"She's almost carried into the Star Room, where there are vases bursting with exotic and brightly coloured flowers. A glass of cava is thrust into her hand, and at once a team of people begin sitting her down in front of a mirror, complimenting and correctifying her makeup at the same time.

"'So pleased to be working with you,' says Rory, the make up guy – who's come from your story, Markmark, changed career and found something else to do – since he couldn't get into that room place and he's given up trying.

"'You are so beeeeeeaaautiful, like a laaaaaaady.' Rory has also started speaking differently – in an attempt to break away from his former life. Two beautiful girls start attending to her feet.

"A balding moustached and big bellied man in a too-tight black t-shirt knocks on the door and enters the changing room.

"'Oh feckerella,' he says. 'You are even more stunning to look at than I thought…My camera's going to love you.'

"'You know,' says Fran, 'it's so nice to be made so welcome, and made to feel such a part of everything. I don't normally get this when I turn up…'

"Just then a guy with model looks and a big bronzed pec-flexing fully shaved chest arrives at the doorway.

"'Hi,' he says, 'should be a good shoot today, I'm feeling good.'

"'Well, good,' says Fran. 'I'm not really used to people making such an effort and I'm so touched, it's a real change for me, you all make me feel so special and wanted and…'

"Then a tall gaunt middle aged man, with white hair, a white goatee beard, TV frame glasses and a black baseball hat with white lettering saying 'AGAIN BABY' pushes his way into the room.

"'Hey, did you get my…you are looking hot today.' He takes a step back, readjusts his glasses and puts them back on over the bridge of his nose.

"'In all the time I've worked with you, you've never looked so…'

"'Natural, like a yoghurt?' offers Rory. English has by now ceased to be his first language.

"'Right. Natural. And it's a quality I've never noticed in you before. Today could be one hell of a shoot.'

"'I hope so,' says Fran. 'How many other auditions are you doing today?'

"'Auditions?' says the director. 'No no no, we're going to shoot the whole thing today.'

'We're filming?' she says.

"Fran looks back at him blankly. She looks at the guy with the shaved brown chest. She looks at the cameraman. She looks at Rory and the two make up assistants who look up from her feet manicures.

"'Lana Lush, you're such a jokey joker,' says Rory. 'You know full well we're doing Anal Space Invasion today.'

"And everyone stops what they're doing and stares right back at Fran."

4

I got up to get some more beers. I dropped two on the kitchen floor and they smashed. I found a dustpan and I cleared it up. The pieces sounded like tiny glass insects scuttling away from me on the floor as I swept them up.

Cab began his story.

"My story, as it turns out, also has Rory in it. Realising he was going nowhere as a make-up guy with English as his third language, he re-learnt English and decided to sail a boat around the world.

"So Rory went to a shop to get some equipment. He gets some sailing gloves, a book on sailing techniques, and a beard trimmer. He's just looking in the equipment cabinet when the sales guy comes up to him and says:

"'I would strongly encourage you to take advantage of our GPSNtials, it's a globally connected satellite tracking system, capable of locating your position anywhere on earth to any height above ground level or up to half a mile below sea level.'

"The sales guy, in his shop t-shirt, sailing trousers and sailing shoes has hardly paused for breath before he continues.

"'The great thing about this particular package is it boasts a direct link up between your signal and a dedicated local rescue back-up unit: they have networks all over the world and they transfer you from unit to unit according to your current position, like a global safety net, I shouldn't really do this, but I can let you have it at 15% off. 20% off, but I can't do anymore than that. 25% and some free socks and another blade for the beard trimmer.'

"So, won over, Rory buys the GPSNtials kit – a black plastic box about the size of a shoebox with a single flashing green light.

"Four weeks into his trip his sailing vessel runs into difficulties, just off the coast of a place he doesn't seem to have a map for. Or, if he does have a map for it, he doesn't recognise where he is. All he can see for miles around is water. He knows for sure he's either in the Atlantic or the Pacific Ocean. Or a mile from the Isle of Wight.

"In the night, in rough seas biting at the sides of his stricken vessel, his ship begins to take on water. Rory is forced to bail out. He gets himself and as many provisions as he can, into the small orange dingy. He also brings with him the small black plastic box with the flashing green light.

"Rory is adrift for what he thinks are days, but he loses all track of time, falling in and out of consciousness in the relentless sun and frazzling heat.

"One morning he wakes with a bump. His first reaction is to snap his limbs up tight, thinking it could be a shark. Then, as he opens his eyes, he thinks a rescue ship might finally have found him. However, as his eyes begin to focus, he realises that it's another orange dingy, about the same size as his own. There is someone inside. They are dazed and mostly unconscious, with a large unruly dark brown beard. They are doing worse than him. Rory helps his new companion drink, and feeds him a survival biscuit.

"When he comes to, introductions are made with the grim sense of humour familiar to all people who share these situations. Rory learns that Geoff, for 'tis his name, has been adrift for four months. Geoff gives Rory a tour of his dingy. They both attempt to make the tour last as long as they can.

"'Oh,' says Rory, 'I see you have one of these too,' pointing at the black plastic box about the size of a shoebox. But its flashing green light isn't flashing. It's off.

"'How come yours isn't on?' says Rory.

"'Because the battery ran out,' explains Geoff, scratching his long, tree-like beard.

"'But I thought they had a six month life on them.'

"'Oh, they do,' says Geoff, finding something in his beard, smelling it, then eating it.

"'Oh right,' says Rory, unsure. 'Well, mine's still good for a while and we've plenty of food and water. If the weather's good to us we ought to be able to hold out for the rescue team.'

"'Oh,' says Geoff, suddenly perking up and looking Rory straight in the eyes, 'but I am the rescue team.'"

5

It was starting to get late by now, and the prospect of checking out at twelve the next day was starting to loom. Wood knocked the puttering candle over in an attempt to revive it and a small fire started behind the sofa.

"Oh sheeet!" yelled Hassan. "We're arsonists! We're arsonists!"

The fire started lapping at the back of the sofa, roaring up an instant heat. Cab threw his beer over it and put it out.

Hassan began his story with only three candles, accompanied by the smell of scorched carpet and spilt beer.

"Well, this is a story about Rory," he said, "way before that, back when he was still at school, just about to leave and do other stuff.

"Now Rory, like his three friends, Cory, Tori, and Tobermory, had basically nothing to do. They used to spend their time sitting on walls flicking V signs at passing cars or going down to the park to talk about how bored they were. I mean, these people had absolutely nothing to do, and none of them were capable of forming the first idea of a future any of them could have. Every day seemed to have the same familiar kind of 'uhu – now what' quality that every other previous day also had. They got up, they watched daytime TV, they had a wank, they went through their rooms for stuff to sell, they sold some stuff, they went to places where one milkshake would take an hour and a half to drink, they went to internet cafes and found sites with kittens playing rock music, and they rented videos, and they stayed round each others' houses and they didn't go to sleep because there was no point in going to sleep, and they didn't get up because there was no point in getting up.

"One day one of them had the brilliant idea of going round the posh estate and throwing stones at the windows. They all instantly knew this was an idea of genius.

"At the first house they picked up small stones from the pavement and hurled them at the windows facing the road.

"A man in a wannabe football manager's sheepskin coat comes out soon after and yells: 'clear off, clear off the lot of ya.'

"So they go to the second house, pick up some stones and start throwing them. After only a few stones have hit they hear the wild barks of several dogs and a guy in a black shell suit and non-exercise body bursts out of the house, seems to struggle to restrain several dogs from behind the front door, then screams: 'if you little fuckers ever come back and ever ever do that again I'll set my dogs on you, and me and them'll make such a mess of you... as you will *never ever* forget as long as you live and breathe.'

"So they moved on, and went to the third house in the estate. Again, they picked up some small stones from the pavement and started throwing them at the windows of the house, though by now it was a little more half-hearted.

"A mother in an apron and rigid set hair came out and shouted loudly, but clearly: 'please go away, you naughty naughty people, you.'

"So they stopped throwing the stones and the woman went in. Then they all looked at each other, and they could tell they all thought the same thing at the same time.

"'Back to the second one?' said Rory, and they all nodded heads in agreement and picked up the biggest stones they could find on their way there."

6

I woke in the morning with the sting of a white sky and the swamp of beer in my hungover head. A bleached out Hassan was by the window, the curtain puller opener culprit.

"Markmark!" he said.

"Whatwhat?"

"Looklook!"

It was the kind of featureless white winter sky you could just drift up into and no one would be able to stop you and probably no one would ever see you again, and they'd say, 'oh yes, I remember them, last time I saw them it was that empty white sky day'. Then Hassan directed my attention to the ground. It was like a block white colour fill in Photoshop.

7

The four of us had been walking through the snow for about an hour. The snow was as white as new polystyrene packaging and just as crunchy, but without the squeak. The whole Earth had that un-smell of freshness and cold.

Then we came to a small footbridge. We stood on it and looked down. We could see the imprints of four people who'd done flat fixed star jump shapes in the snow, arms and legs out wide. Whoever they were had walked to the bank from the path back by the trees on the other side and laid down in the untouched snow, then walked back retracing their steps, pretty accurately, so there was almost only one set for each shape. Only the occasional double heel gave it away.

We all looked at the four shapes for a while, not saying much, just looking, thinking our own thoughts, in the cold air with the empty sky all around us.

The drive back. Work tomorrow. Are reunions a bad idea because they can't ever live up to ridiculous expectations? How can you keep your friends? How can you let them know that you think about them? How can you let them know how much better everything is because of them? Stuck in a job. Career change. Wrong decisions. Feeling nowhere. Nowhereness. Not even in it, just drifting above it. Not expecting the world to be so indifferent to us. Not even indifference with any sense of the extreme. Feeling dirty from failure. Dirty from the inability to visualise what success would be. If snow was black we wouldn't crave it so much. It wouldn't make our lives feel clean. It's because it's white we need it. It makes us feel we can begin again, new and fresh and full of hope.

Hassan said, "follow me." No one asked why. We all just did. It was a flock of birds moment. If one bird goes the rest just follow.

We walked back to the path by the trees – having to loop round them from the other way we'd come. We stood facing the four lines of footprints. Hassan looked round at us then put a foot into the nearest print. Slowly at first. Then the second step was faster, third faster still. He turned round again, and Wood, then me and Cab, both took a set of footprints each. We all trod in them as best we could, trying to stay within the sides. We followed them as they took us down the side of the bank near the footbridge, leading us to one star jump body shape each. Hassan first, then all of us, manoeuvred ourselves into the readymade shape in the snow, being careful not to ruin the sides. We sunk down as low into the snow as we could. Then we stared up at the empty white sky, feeling like blocks slotted into the right holes in a children's toy.

Things You Can Buy

1. Single Deck Cassette Recorder
Best thing ever. Best present ever. By miles.
I can record anything I like. Hear tapes. Don't have many tapes.
Ohohohohoh, that song I like. Quick, a blank tape.
Don't record over that one.
Press play and record together.
Did I get more than 30 seconds of it?
Be better prepared, get the tape ready just in case in future.
Age: 10
Ambition: Be a DJ.

2. SLR Camera
A proper camera. Like grown ups have.
Best to get a grown up to help when you put the film in.
You must never open the back or you ruin your pictures.
Be still or you make the picture blurry.
Take lens cap off.
You can just see a thing and press and you have a photograph.
You can keep photographs for ever.
Age: 11
Ambition: Be a photographer.

3. CD player
For my room.
On my own.
Age: 13
Ambition: Listen to music.

4. Personal Walkman
For the bus.
On my own.
Between lessons.
Age: 14
Ambition: Be in a band.

5. Home Computer
Tape screech for loading.
MS DOS.
Text based adventures.
Age: 16
Ambition: Play computer games.

6. TV
Where's the dopper?
Channel hopping.
Making sentences from channel hopping.
Turn it down.
Turn it up.
Soaps.
Sitcoms.
Reality Shows
News.
Adverts.
Documentaries.
Age: 17
Ambition: Come up with ideas for TV shows.

7. VHS player
Wind it on.
Set the timer.
Wind it back.
Write on it or you'll forget.
Age: 19
Ambition: Spend all day in bed watching videos.

8. Mobile Phone
Incoming call.
I'm in a shop!
Txt me.
Missed call.
Battery low.
Voicemail.
That ringtone is still in my head.
Age: 24
Ambition: Smash up phone.

9. Games Console
New game.
Save.
Load.
One last try.
Cheatcodes.
Age: 25
Ambition: Beat friends at chosen game in large competition with drinks and snacks.

10. APS Camera
You sure these will catch on?
Age: 26
Ambition: Sell SLR camera.

11. New computer
Modem.
Printer.
Email.
Hard drive.
Internet.
Age: 27
Ambition: Leave work, something not computer based. Have children?

Maurice Suckling

12. Digital Camera
Memory card.
Zoom.
Pixels.
Download.
Delete.
Attach.
Age: 28
Ambition: Sell APS camera, and digital camera, and leave work. Have children?

13. DVD player
Sharp image.
Chapter skip.
Extra features.
Remastered.
Age: 31
Ambition: Live in small house by sea and grow own food, pick olives, read books and have no access to phones or computers.

14. PDA
Wireless.
Handheld.
Email.
Phone.
Age: 35
Ambition: Can no longer think of one.

THE AMAZING ADVENTURES OF NO ONE IN PARTICULAR

Episode 2

On the train a woman came along with the refreshments trolley.

I was tempted.

But the prices were so high it annoyed me.

So I went back to looking out the window.

The two blokes behind me were talking ...

...about when one of them nearly hit a deer.

It made me think about what happened with James and me that time.

We did some work for his uncle in the summer between school and university.

He had a big white van.

We drove the van for him to collect and deliver tools.

James' uncle's business was in the country. The country roads were bendy.

There were often stories of people seeing and nearly hitting deer.

I was driving as James was telling me how his uncle once hit and killed a deer.

They brought the deer back to his garage in pieces and tried to put it back together.

Then a deer ran out in front of us.

We hit it.

We rushed out the van to see if it was OK.

It was alive, but bleeding everywhere.

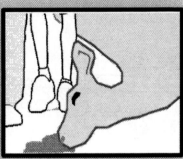

James made a suggestion.

We looked in the van for what tools to use.

We found a hammer ...

... and a saw ...

... and a nail gun.

Worst of three coins and I got the job.

I put the nail gun to its head, fired twice and it died.

We went to lift the deer off the road.

Then we found we had nailed it to the tarmac.

To be continued ...

59

Part Three

The Seventh Colour

Seven colours exist that can never be reproduced. Six have never been seen. One of these colours – the colour itself, not a reproduction – has been seen just once. In Paris in 1883 a man in his late forties drained chemicals from a fixing tray. The developed image in this tray was a photograph, one of a number in a series of time tests. On this image, in the eyes of a woman at a railway station, was the colour.

The photographer was too hasty and failed to check the image in daylight. In the red glow of his studio the colour was un-noticeable and indistinguishable from the other tones.

He would never know, but the colour remained on that photograph, kept in a drawer, until a fire in 1940. Yet even if he, or anyone else had ever seen this colour, it is unlikely it would have been recognised for what it was. Its light frequency was *precisely* the colour of intimacy.

Televisionism

1

I once had a girlfriend who was famous. I suppose she still is in a way, but I can't really say she's my girlfriend anymore. At least we don't go out and we don't see each other, and people tend to see that as significant. Maybe she's not even actually famous anymore either. I doubt anyone much under 15 has heard of her, and there're still some people much older who'd have no idea who you were talking about, not that I ever mention it. If anyone ever brings up the subject it's never me. That would be like giving a little piece of her away each time, and where she is now I can't get anymore of her so I have to look after what I have left. Not that she's dead, or anything like that. Not exactly

But the people who do know about her, who do remember, all saw the same TV programme. It's been shown on repeats plenty of times, but it's never had the same impact on people as it did the first time, the time it went out live. It was one of those in-the-moment things; one of those this-was-the-year-that... kind of things. It's six years since it happened, and there's still people, who saw it live, who talk about it like they permanently carry the experience of watching it around with them.

My girlfriend was called Ciara. (Say *was*? Say *is*?) We met in a bar early evening, when I'd just popped in with some people from work. It was a Wednesday, and I usually only drank with them for one or two on a Friday. I was at the bar getting drinks when I was tapped on the shoulder. I turned round and there was Ciara. She was standing in front of a lamp by the wall, so her whole head had this strange glow of light all around it. With the bar being low lit and her face being the wrong side of that light, I suppose it should have been harder to make out her features than it was, though I didn't think about that at the time. Her sharp blue almost luminous eyes seemed to go right through my own eyes and play ping pong all round the inside of my head. She looked like the kind of person who could be famous. People that good looking can always get famous. I suppose her hair should have been in shadow and not been so bright and blonde nor emitting the kind of hazy radiant gold-tinged glow either.

I realised that not only was I staring, but that also she was trying to hand me something; a mobile phone.

My mobile phone. I hadn't even got halfway through my confused expression before she spoke.

"That's right, it's your phone. You're going to need it if I'm going to call you."

I thanked her and asked if I'd dropped it.

"Oh no," she said, "I just magic'd it out of your pocket."

I thanked her again and picked up my previous expression from where I'd left off and kept it going for just under a week.

She did call. It was just under a week later. We arranged to meet at the same pub. We got our drinks and got the last free seats in the place at a table, just as it was starting to fill up.

I had an older brother and a younger sister. She had an older sister and a younger brother. We both worked as junior producers in advertising firms. We'd both been there coming up to three years each. Our favourite band was the same, our favourite film was the same, our favourite place in the whole city to watch the world go by was the same.

It was my turn to go to the bar. The pub was heaving right then and it must have been three ranks deep, maybe four in places. Ciara must've seen the look in my eyes.

"I'll get them," she said.

"No, no, it's my round," I insisted. I didn't want her to think I wasn't a drinks buyer.

"No really – look at it," she said. "Close your eyes."

"What?"

"Close your eyes."

I shot a few looks to the side, not sure what she was up to.

"Close your eyes," she said, in a voice that made me want to.

So I closed my eyes and before I'd barely had time to smile at the thought of how I must look, she told me to open them.

There, in front of us were two fresh and pint-full glasses of beer.

"Howdyou do that?" I said.

"Magic," she said.

2

We met up next at a restaurant. I had the task of choosing so it was important to get the balance right between effort and over-fancy. I went for a low lit bistro friends had told me about but I'd never tried. Ciara and I both chose the same starter and main course, and we shared a bottle of wine. She picked it, but it was the one I was just about to mention.

The second bottle of wine came.

"Jim, what do you actually believe in?"

"Err, the same as you?" I tried.

"And what is that, then, do you think?"

I overfilled both glasses slightly, as the young so-Italian waiter cleared the table next to us.

"You know, the usual, don't do stuff to people you wouldn't want done to you…don't litter…and don't drink milk past it's sell by date."

The waiter backed into us by accident, spun round and lost control of his arm-balanced plates as they crashed onto our table, sending my wine glass over my clean and specially ironed white shirt. The waiter began apologising. It takes me twenty-five minutes to do a shirt.

"No, no, it's fine," I said.

The stain looked the size of two hands splayed out, one on top of the other. He started setting things right on our table and picking the glass up.

"I sorry, I sorry, I sort it for you."

"No, really, it's fine," said Ciara, standing up and helping to brush me down. She seemed to pick up a cloth that the waiter had dropped, though it was hard to tell in that light and it was so fast. I saw her wipe at my shirt a couple of times as I was sitting back down.

"No, it's fine, Ciara, it's fine. Don't worry about that."

I sat back down and the waiter continued picking things up and apologising and offering to pay for the shirt to be cleaned.

"No, don't worry about that," I said, and looked down and saw that the stain wasn't there at all. Then I looked back at Ciara.

Maurice Suckling

Whenever she touched me it felt like my sense of touch, which must have been usually set at somewhere between 1 and 2 on the dial, had been spun right round as far as it would go. I could feel everything much more, like every cell in my skin had grown tiny microscopic hands of their own. Like all my nerve endings were much closer the surface than ever before. If she put her hand on my skin it almost felt like it hurt and it made my whole body shudder. I used to ask her to do it as often as possible. Sometimes she'd wait till I stopped shaking till she did it again.

We kissed for the first time that night. I thought maybe my head was on fire, but in a way that I liked. I tried to stop it shaking by putting both my hands round it. It made my hands hot.

A month after that we went to the theatre together for the first time. At the door they were taking tickets and tearing them. I put my hand in my jacket pocket and had one of those busy hands, empty head moments. Before my hands had given up I'd already come to picture the two tickets left in my flat in the kitchen in the special *Do Not Forget These* place by the kettle I'd put them in. I was about to explain to Ciara, but she could already tell from my face.

"Doesn't matter," she said, and walked me towards the door. From her pocket she pulled out two tickets, looking just like the ones I'd left behind, handed them over to the ticket woman, who put a rip in them and handed them back to Ciara. Ciara put them back in her pocket then we went in to see the play. Bits of it were pretty good, but I couldn't really concentrate on it.

Ciara had to go back to her place after coz she had to be up extra early for work in the morning – we'd got the tickets a while before and the original plan was to stay someplace near the theatre, but we'd had to shelve that plan. The taxi took her back to her place first. She apologised again as she got out and I told her it didn't matter as it wasn't her fault. Then the taxi dropped me off at my flat. As soon as I got in I walked straight through to the kitchen and found the tickets just where I'd left them. They both had rips in them.

I didn't want to phone her because she'd be trying to get to sleep for her early morning, so I sent Ciara a text telling her I thought she should be on television.

3

I'd warned Ciara about my mum's cooking, but she was sporting enough to come for dinner anyway. My mum and dad were delighted to see her, and they did these little approval looks to each other when they thought no one else could see. Living together for such a long time must somehow dull your awareness of other people being around.

"So you do the same work as James, is that right?" said my dad, helping himself to the rice. My mother, thinking Ciara sounded foreign, had cooked an Indian meal, at least she called it Indian. Once when my mum had tried cooking a Chinese meal for Chinese New Year I didn't eat another one for nearly two months. It used to be my favourite food.

"Sort of," said Ciara, "but I'm thinking of doing something else."

"Mum! What have you done? This tastes absolutely amazing!" I'd just had my first tentative helping of korai lamb. Usually the names of my mum's dishes were loose clues more than direct answers.

"Thank you James," she said. "It did work out rather better than I was expecting, didn't it."

"Mum, this could be in a restaurant!" I said. And then I remembered seeing Ciara disappear into the kitchen a little earlier when my mum had come into the lounge with drinks.

"Like what?" said my dad, who didn't seem to notice anything unusual in the food. I think his taste buds had been systematically eradicated over the years so that he could now only differentiate foods by size and colour.

"Like what? What are you going to do instead?" pressed my Dad, interested.

"Oh, well I'm hoping Jim's going to be able to come along with me to find out," she said.

And I did.

We both had to take the Friday afternoon off work. I'd tried getting clues from her about what we were doing but she refused to tell me anything. Maybe I could've guessed from the tube stop we met at.

At the security gate she said we had an appointment and they let us through.

"We?"

"Well, no, just me, really, but I wanted you to come along too."

We walked through to reception and I waited while Ciara spoke to the people there. We took a lift to the fourth floor and followed the red signs along the cream coloured corridors. We were told to wait on a brown leather sofa in a secretary's office. There were awards and photos of famous people all around the walls.

When it was our turn to go in Ciara led the way. She shook hands with Mr Jeremies and introduced me as her manager, which was the first I'd heard of it. Mr Jeremies, curly black hair, dark features and exec-shaped body, stepped back into the room and perched on the front edge of his large desk, looking towards us.

"So…" he said, and held his palms up, like he was waiting for something. "Show me something. A trick. A card trick or something."

Ciara stepped forwards and held out both hands, as if she wanted him to count how many fingers. She then turned and showed them to me, so I could see. The same number as usual.

"Mr Jeremies, would you please take a card from the deck," and she gestured to the deck that neither I, nor Mr Jeremies from his expression, had noticed on his desk before. Then he recovered himself and pulled a wry face. He picked up the cards and seemed to spend a while looking through them, turning them upside down and glancing at some of the backs.

"If you could choose a card, show it to my manager, but not let me see it, please."

Again, Mr Jeremies had this wry look, and again he seemed to take a while to look through the cards.

"It's a full deck, Mr Jeremies, not doctored in any way."

He smiled back at her; wry, once again. Then as he chose a card Ciara closed her eyes put her hands over them and turned her head away. It was a Queen of Diamonds. Then he put it back in the deck.

"You want the deck back now?" he said.

Ciara turned round and opened her eyes.

"No thank you. You can keep them."

There was a moment's pause in the room and I couldn't hear anything right then, no sounds of traffic on the nearby roads, no sounds of people in corridors, no office sounds at all.

"So are you going to tell me my card then?" he said.

"This is your card," said Ciara, and held up her left hand to show him her palm.

He folded his arms and rocked back slightly where he was, then looked at her more closely. Ciara spun round to show me the Queen of Diamonds perfectly drawn on the palm of her hand.

"The card itself, Mr Jeremies, is in the CD-tray of your computer."

He blinked at her, then walked round to the back of his desk, pressed a button on his desktop pc. I heard the whine of it opening. He didn't move for a moment or so. Then he picked out the card and held it up. The Queen of Diamonds. He looked past me in the doorway, out to his secretary, flashing suspicious look.

"Card tricks…," said Mr Jeremies dismissively.

"It's not really card tricks I want to do," said Ciara.

"So what would you do if I gave you a show?" said Mr Jeremies, for the first time sounding like he was warming to her, opening up and becoming interested.

"Why don't you call my agent and we can discuss it," she said, then threw all the cards into the air and the whole deck stuck face to the ceiling, so all the patterned red backs of the cards were showing and arranged into shapes giving out a string of numbers. She didn't even stay long enough to see the effect, she walked past me on her way out as I was still staring upwards.

"I didn't know you had an agent," I said as we got back into the lift.

"Oh well…there's lots you don't know about me, Jim."

Then she kissed me until the lift came to a stop and we both opened our eyes and she was laughing and holding my pants in her hand. My vision was a little blurred by the quivering but I reached down and could feel my trousers were still on, fully buttoned, and zipped up.

4

Things were still going well between us as Ciara started filming for her show. It was going to come out in six half hour episodes to be shown late at night. When Ciara worked late we used to get cabs back from the studio. Every time we got lucky as soon as we left the building and a taxi had either just dropped someone off at the front doors, or was just driving by on the main road with its light on. We would go for something to eat in restaurants that were still open even though it was so late, or so early, and we would frequently be the only people eating there. Sometimes she would reach across and put her hand near mine. Sometimes she would make her hand touch. This was messy if I was eating soup.

One particular night we got back to her flat late and she had a line of twelve tea lights on the windowsill. She clicked her fingers and all twelve lit at once. It was very romantic and I was about to take her clothes off when I realised she didn't have any on. I was about to take my own off when I realised I didn't have any on either. We couldn't have slept more than four hours that night. I woke up with a bruise on the back of my head. Ciara said I'd been shaking and my head had knocked against the metal headboard for a couple of hours but I looked so peaceful she didn't want to move me.

Now I think about it, I never once had an orgasm when she didn't have one at the same time. That ought to have made it absolutely clear to me what was going on. But it didn't. I am a bit slow that way, and probably a bit quick the other.

The Ciara Wilson Show was enjoyed by students, insomniacs, shift workers and people who were tired and had already decided to go to bed, but didn't turn the TV off in time and so got caught.

She and the producers had decided to go for a reality TV, this is really real, type of approach. In the first episode she took her ever-present camera crew into a shopping centre. She stopped a couple in their 20s, all dressed up in high street designer wear, weighed down with shopping bags and asked them if she could show them some magic. When they said she could, she took out a £20 note from her pocket and asked the woman, called Jenny, to write her name on it in lipstick. She wore an *Estee Lauder Hot Copper*. Ciara then asked if Jenny had recently bought anything that they'd wrapped up in front of her in a shop. Stacey told her there were a couple of things. Some *Clinique* perfume for a friend and some *Body Shop* soaps for her mum. Ciara asked Jenny to make a choice between them. She chose the soap. Ciara asked her to open it, and Jenny went into her bag, took the package out, moved the green ribbon to one side and carefully unwrapped it. There was the soap, still in its tight cellophane wrapper. Jenny looked up puzzled.

"Turn it over," said Ciara.

And inside the heat-sealed cellophane, in contact with the soap, tightly folded, was a £20 note. When Jenny opened it she found the note had her lipstick signature on it. Jenny and her boyfriend, who remained known as Boyfriend, looked stunned. Ciara handed a package to Jenny that looked like the one just opened.

"One with its wrapper still on," said Ciara.

There was a lot of this kind of stuff across the whole six episodes.

She took her camera crew into a pub. She made a pint of beer travel the length of a bar to a gawping group of lads. It hovered head height through the air and she didn't spill a drop.

She took her crew into a park at night. She said there was a rain cloud just above her head, just out of reach if she tried to jump up to it. You couldn't really see anything because it was so dark. She explained it was a cumulus cloud, though much lower than usual. She then clicked her fingers and the rain started pouring over her, soaking her, but nothing around her – just her. She proceeded to walk around in the otherwise dry park and it seemed as if the cloud followed her wherever she went, until she was utterly drenched.

In her last show she went into a restaurant and appeared to change someone's leftover desert into a birthday cake. When the birthday person said she couldn't eat the cake because she was too full, Ciara suggested she at least cut into it because the birthday person's house keys were inside. On cutting into the cake the birthday person discovered not only was this true, but that there was also a specific Cretan earring to replace the one she'd been upset about losing earlier in the evening. In the shock she knocked her glass onto the floor. Ciara reached down onto the ground, gathered all the pieces together, seemed to throw them into the air and caught a fully formed wine glass. Almost fully formed, there was a tiny chip in the lip of the glass. Ciara reached down again, found a piece of glass no bigger than the stud of the replacement earring. She seemed to do no more than touch it to the glass, and the glass was fully repaired, you couldn't see any cracks or repair lines in it anywhere.

TV programmes and internet sites were rife with speculation as to how she made the tricks work and the complex research and preparation that must have to go into each one. I surprised Ciara with a cup of tea and caught her scrolling through a website one afternoon, looking scowly.

"They think they can work out how it's done." She sounded hurt.

"Well…," I said, "that's a good thing, isn't it. It creates a buzz."

"You're right," she said and put her hand on mine and looked musing out of the window at the road below, then noticed I was spilling hot tea over my leg and whimpering.

As a result of the success of the show Ciara was invited on to a talk show program. She looked unbelievable in a black dress with a low V down her cleavage, showing off her naturally dark and inviting skin. As her manager I naturally wanted the interview to go well. As her boyfriend I wanted her to turn around before she got to the bottom of the stairs and get straight into a cab with me.

When the talk show host asked, without really expecting an answer, how she managed to do the tricks she did, she looked him straight in the eyes and said 'because I am magic.' Even if you'd never seen her show you'd agree just by seeing her in that dress.

The host pressed her some more about the ways she did things. She agreed to show him a trick then and there. He suggested a card trick.

"You people always want card tricks," she mused, good naturedly.

"You say that like you're not one of us," said the host, chuckling.

"Oh, I'm not," she said. "Not exactly. I am, but I'm also something else." She was looking at him seriously now. She looked amazing in that dress.

"And what would that be…magic? I suppose." He chuckled, bringing the studio audience with him.

"Sort of." She smiled and nodded sincerely. The audience laughed. She looked amazing in that dress.

She asked the host to take the pack of cards from his top pocket. A pack he didn't know he had there. She asked him to pick a card and show the audience and the camera. The Three of Clubs.

She asked him to put the card back in the pack, and then hand the pack to her. Once he did, she took them and then threw them into the air. All the cards disappeared, as if they'd been sucked in to a specific invisible point. The audience applauded.

Ciara then asked the host to pick up the egg he was sitting on. He didn't know he was sitting on one. The audience applauded. As he held it in his hands it began to crack and a tiny hairless, slightly alien looking chick emerged. There was something in its beak. Ciara took hold of the bird and extracted the thing from its beak. She unrolled it. It was the Three of Clubs. The audience applauded. From out of the space where the deck of cards had disappeared, out of nothing but the air, there suddenly appeared a small red-brown kestrel with something in its mouth. It came and rested on Ciara's free hand and fed the chick. The audience went quiet, too stunned to know what they were seeing. She looked amazing in that dress. A patter of applause broke out into a run.

That night's lovemaking was the most intense so far. I asked her to keep the dress on. She wanted me to pull her hair and call her magic. By the digital clock at the side of her bed it was 4.32am when we finished making love. I was lying in bed in the same position we'd stopped in, with my eyes still open staring blankly at the clock at 11.08am, when I finally stopped shaking.

After the talk show the TV company asked Ciara back for another series. We went to their offices and she explained that she might consider it. But before that she wanted to do something else. She wanted a *Ciara Wilson Special*.

"And what are you going to do with that?" asked Mr Jeremies.

"Something special," said Ciara, plainly.

"Like what?"

"Explain to people who I am," she said.

5

I never liked the idea for this show and I told her. I didn't like anything to do with guns. But she insisted this was the right trick to do on the show and, what was more, it had to be done live if there was any point doing it at all. The TV channel weren't sure, but Ciara managed to persuade them she could make it work. In the end, they agreed and paid for us to shoot the show overseas, to get over the legal problems with filming the show in this country.

The large posters went up in city centres, the papers talked it up, the TV stings appeared and the date got closer and closer. On the plane over to the studio specially prepared for us I told Ciara she really didn't have to go through with this. I told her there was still time to change the trick she was going to do. Part of the appeal in the media had been that she hadn't said what the trick was actually going to be. She said it involved her and a gun, and that the outcome would be magic, but that was all.

She touched my hand, made me spill my in-flight white wine all over my lap, and told me she really did have to go through with it, because it was time that people knew.

"Knew what?" I said, feeling just how cold the wine was in my lap.

"Knew about me," she said, and turned to look out of the window. There was a thick snowscape of clouds just underneath our plane and the sun was high and bright. When we'd left the ground it had been a horrible dark, rain-dreary day. Now we were above the weather, like we lived in paradise, or were at least visiting until we had to land.

The Ciara Wilson Special went out live at 8pm GMT. In it Ciara wore a stunning, plummeting neckline white dress which went as far as her belly button, in which she wore a simple single fake diamond stud. I had bought it for her – I couldn't afford real diamonds, but she said she liked it more than real ones because they were common.

Ciara was on stage for just under an hour. There were two 28 minute sections broken by adverts for *Audis, Clios, IBM, Oil of Olay, L'Oreal*, and a psycho thriller released on DVD in between.

In the first half she explained that she was going to show that she was, in fact, actually magic. She was going to stand opposite the large revolver on the stand at the opposite end of the stage. The gun somehow resembled an angry parrot. Other than that the stage was almost bare. The only other thing on it was a backdrop of a large projector screen, which showed no image at all.

The first half involved lots of checking of the gun, of its sights and the lethal quality of the bullets it fired, how it wasn't connected to any remote apparatus and all that. It also involved finding a volunteer from the audience, a man in a blue shirt called Gary, who was given a sealed white envelope by Ciara. She explained that no matter what happened in the second half of the show Gary was to read out this envelope and it would all make some kind of sense.

She looked amazing in that dress.

In the adverts Ciara was backstage, alone in her room in the dark, sitting cross-legged on the floor. The door was slightly open and I watched her breathing slowly in and out in the slice of light from the corridor. I left her as long as I could. One of the stand-by medics walked past the door and the sound seemed to disrupt her. She opened her eyes and looked at me. I shuffled a couple of steps closer and was about to speak.

"I know," she said, in a voice that made me feel like I didn't need to say anything anymore. She jumped up and her eyes looked exhilarated, somehow bluer and brighter even in the dark room. She snapped a quick kiss on my lips and it stung my mouth like static.

Like the professional she had now become, Ciara built up the tension in the second half whilst doing little more than recapping what she'd said before. Finally she stood in position with the angry parrot pointing straight at her beautiful face on the other side of the stage.

"The real beauty of this is the simplicity of it," she said.

"In a moment, at my command, a bullet will shoot out of the gun straight towards me. As we have already seen, I have no wires and no wireless connections to the gun. As we already know, the gun has been checked, its sights tested, the bullets tested, and there is no one else controlling the gun, or able to control the gun from off-stage. There is also no one else able to control the bullet once it has left the gun."

The lights dimmed. The sound dropped out of the studio, apart from my heart, which sounded as loud as a drill. This all happening live, being beamed out to millions of people watching back at home, was generating a strange, intense buzz inside the studio.

I saw her lips move. "Fire."

The bullet seemed to take so long to reach her. I had time to think, will she catch it in her teeth? Will the bullet turn into a butterfly halfway? Will she say 'stop' and make it hang in mid air? Why wouldn't she tell me what the trick was?

Then the bullet struck her and she collapsed. Blood seeped from her head before anyone could take in what had happened. A woman in the audience shrieked. The lights went on. Panic and uncertainty, and the show was still live on air.

Ciara's body was rushed off stage. I was kept away by the medics as they put her on the stretcher in the ambulance. Because I was back stage I didn't see this at the time, but the floor manager came on stage, calmed people as best he could and asked for the guy in the audience, Gary, to bring his envelope on stage. Gary, visibly shaking as he tried to open the envelope, took out a piece of paper, and in a deep, faintly stuttering, estuary English accent, read out:

"Sorry if I've shocked anyone but really there's not the slightest need to worry, because I should be appearing via the pre-arranged CCTV connection beaming live from the ambulance."

The screen at the back of the stage suddenly blinked on displaying images, hard to make out in the studio lights. The lights were cut. Grainy black and white, slightly jerky images appeared to show Ciara's inert body, medics attending to her.

Gary read on:

"I am actually dead right at this moment. The bullet entered my brain causing devastating, instant damage. Then passed right through my head to the other side. Medics attending to me now will be able to verify that I am technically, medically, actually dead.
I will however, leave the ambulance in the next 10 seconds and magic myself back into the studio, alive."

Gary stepped away from the stage as he looked over his shoulder and the audience noticed the timer in the top right of the screen, picking up the count down from 5.

4.

3.

2.

1.

Ciara ripped through the projector screen and stood there, arms out wide, beaming a wide, toothy smile, a small red mark on her forehead in the close up.

The audience were silent. I have never known a room so stunned. The recording shows it took twenty-four seconds for the applause to start. It felt like that in minutes.

6

Ciara said she had a headache that night. Sometimes she said it was at the front of her head, sometimes the back, never consistent. I suspected she was using it as an excuse. I could tell something wasn't right. We spoke little right after the show and slept in separate bedrooms.

The next morning Ciara came into my room with a coat on, newspapers under her arms and a suitcase in each of her thick gloved hands.

"Morning," I said croakily, in what I hoped was a forgiving voice.

"Jim, I have to go," she said.

"Sure, give me ten minutes and we're gone." I said it, but my body hadn't moved.

"No, Jim. I mean me, not us."

"What are you talking about?" Now my body moved and I was half dressed by the time I'd got over to her at the door.

"They didn't get it," she said, dropping her suitcases to the floor either side of her.

She flung the papers on the bed.

"You're on the front page!" I picked through the papers, not able to take everything in.

"They think the medics were in on it. They think the footage of me in the ambulance was someone else."

"You're on the front page!"

"Jim, I have to go." The tone in her voice made me stop.

"What's this got to do with us?"

"Do you think I'm magic?" she said.

I looked in her eyes as hard as I could, even though it seemed to hurt to look. I thought carefully, and answered as definitively as I could.

"Yes."

She grabbed a hug and kissed me on the lips, stopped my head from shaking by holding it still with her thick gloved hands and stepped away.

"Then you understand what I have to do then," she said.

"Do I?"

"Yes," she said, "another way, or another time," and she picked up her suitcases and stepped away.

I felt something in my hand, looked down, opened it up and saw a blunted silver bullet with its head smashed, rolling in my palm.

Ciara left. I still have the bullet.

This Is Not A Virus (Or Is It?)

From: spoofmaster@spooferama.com
Sent: 23 June 2170 00:01
Subject: this is not a virus (or is it?)
Attachment: Virus?

I am assured this story is true. A chicken once lived for years after its head was cut off. The blood around its neck congealed and clotted and it didn't die. It is a testimony to how little of importance is really in a chicken's head that it was able to walk around and do most of the things it always had done. The farmer fed it with a lipped jug and a pipette through the open hole in its neck. It frequently walked into things but was otherwise able to socialise as before.

I think of chickens often. I think of how that one is like human beings after they exchanged God for technology. I think of how somewhere there are millions of chopped off chicken heads in piles with their eyes staring blankly open. And I think of how the chickens with their heads still on are no smarter – just fed simpler.

Download your conscience with technology.
Do you think this is a virus?
Open the attachment and find out.

THE AMAZING ADVENTURES OF NO ONE IN PARTICULAR

Episode 3

Then we heard a car coming.

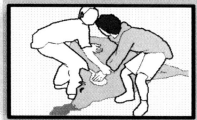

We didn't know what to do .

So we legged it back to the van.

And drove away.

When the train pulled up at the stop I got off.

I walked out of the station and wondered what to do next.

I found the High Street

Someone was dressed in Shakespeare gear handing out leaflets for a play.

I didn't want to see a play.

The last time I dressed up was with James and Jess.

James went as Ghandi, Jess as Princess Leia, I went as John McEnroe.

Also at the party were the Blues Brothers ...

...Elvis, of course...

Einstein and two Audrey Hepburns...

... three Britney Spears in school uniform...

... and Darth Vader.

There was lots of drinking.

Darth Vader hit on Princess Leia.

Ghandi asked him to back off.

He did.

There was more drinking.

Darth Vader came back.

Ghandi told him to back off.

Darth Vader
stayed where he was.

Ghandi told him to back off.

He didn't.

Ghandi hit Darth Vader.

A week later, James was cycling round Australia. He was sucked under a truck and killed.

I dreamt of him cycling up to heaven. Except I knew he wasn't really anywhere.

To be continued ...

Part Four

Snapshots of Glastonbury 2003

3hrs after putting our tents up

We find Spook's phone and blue sunhat inside his white trainers with what looks like blood smeared across them.

"It is," says Catalina. "Look at it." Catalina gives blood regularly, so I dunno, maybe she thinks she's better at knowing about blood than us. Catalina always kinda takes charge whatever though.

Finn looks. I look.

"This is an excellent development, Matt," says Russ looking at me, his irony voice all thick and deep.

The three of us have been waiting for Spook by the urinals with the blue sides at the far end of the Pyramid stage.

"Bingo," I say, and everyone looks up.

Only it's just someone who looks like Spook from the back, with a white t-shirt and the same colour shorts.

I have a sudden feeling that maybe I was hoping so much it was Spook I nearly changed the person into him, when really they look nothing like Spook and started the day wearing something completely different. Ain't it easy to want something so much you almost make it be real.

On the train on the way there

"Keep it down, I'm reading about the weather," smirks Russ out of a paper then disappears behind it again. Catalina and I look at him. No one has said anything. Russ doesn't like silences.

It's the first time for Russ as well as me.

It's Spook's sixth time. He just carries on looking out of the window. He might have heard, he might have not, but you never know with Spook. The countryside wipes past, all green and treed. Rivers, boats, houses that look right and houses that don't. But with Spook you never know what he's looking at or what he's thinking.

"…but my mum goes to Glastonbury too." A girl in a tie-dyed skirt and a cropped top talks to her friend who is almost exactly the same only there's about 30% more of her, as they walk down the carriage. They already have a seat. Everyone heard them as they'd walked through to the buffet before.

"Oh, but last year…" says her friend as they pass our seats.

"Oh, last year," interrupts the disappearing voice, "it took me weeks to adjust to normal life, it's just so wonderful, everyone's just so…"

They have wellies on.

"Should we have brought wellies?" I ask.

"Maybe," says Catalina, it's her fourth time, "do you have any?"

"No," I say, looking to see if Spook is in the conversation. He isn't.

"Nor do we," says Catalina, "do we?" Catalina always goes out with good looking people.

"No," says Russ, putting the paper down, then frowns at Catalina, "so is this like a pilgrimage to you?" Irony / not irony in his voice? You tell me.

Catalina smiles like she knows what he means. He looks at her like he knows what her smile means back – all this and neither of them says anything. This is the kind of thing I want to have between me and Kiri if things ever work out. Kiri wears little blue trainers with tiny hidden socks inside.

Russ looks at the paper and hums a *Sugarbabes* song. Catalina and I turn to watch the non-stop countryside views, and Spook looks at whatever he looks at. I think about him for a while and wonder what's happening inside his head when his face is glazed over like this. I imagine it's like when you look at the sky at night and get sort of fixed looking at a certain star, just watching it twinkle a little bit, wondering if you're only imagining it twinkling and wondering how far away it is and how long ago it died. But really, I have no idea. Spook is the most b-side person I know; b-sides sort of aren't normal songs, but that makes them better and more special because they're harder to find.

If you live at the beginning of the twenty first century and you grew up without religion you need stuff like Glastonbury to really come through for you. You need a place or an occasion where you can download some belief in something. Just anything at all, really. The more choice we have in TV channels and games consoles the less choice we want in other stuff; we're all pretty pushed for time.

"If it rains," says Spook suddenly, "that's good too. In 97 it was just mud, but everyone was just all together, everyone was all part of the same thing. *Radiohead* headlined that year too; as they played *No Surprises* fireworks went up and burst in time with the xylophone notes. It was the best one ever."

Spook is still looking out of the window. More trees. Everyone likes trees. They make you feel like your planet's still ok.

Getting off the bus from the station

They hand out free white groundsheets with a Vodafone logo and free Orange ponchos. We take them, just in case, but feel a bit like we shouldn't.

"If anyone gets lost," says Catalina, her black hair in bunches, "meet at the meeting point – that's what it's for. Once we've got the tent up we'll meet back there, Spook? You listening?"

"Yes," says Spook, under his faded blue sunhat, looking in a different direction. Spook plays memory chess with his dad. He looks like he's in the middle of a move.

The Darkness 8/10

"Give me a D...Give me an Arkness...what've you got?...The Darkness."

"Take your hands off my woman you mutherfucker...mu-mu-mu-mu-mu-mu-mu-mu-mutherfucker... crazymutherfukerfromhell..."

"Why don't we mark everyone out of 10?" says Russ, swinging the day's newspaper (*The Times*) in its plastic wrapper between his finger and thumb. Russ can do the numbers bit on *Countdown*. He does crosswords too. He even brought a pen with a light on the end just in case he wanted to do crosswords at night.

Maurice Suckling

Message on the tannoy

"Would Spook please go to the Meeting Point. That's a message for Spook. Please go to the Meeting Point as soon as possible. Thank you."

Spook had an epileptic fit once. Just once, years and years ago, when Catalina and I were all at school with him. It makes you wonder. It makes you wonder lots of things.

"Worth a try," says Catalina as Russ and I look at her. Catalina has three small silver hoops in each of her ears.

The Inspiral Carpets 7/10

The keyboardist: "Is there anyone here at their first festival? Put your hand up if this is your first festival...here, that kid in the blue top – give him a round of applause – imagine being in his shoes, it's fucking beautiful, man."

The singer: "It's a fucking beautiful sight seeing you all listening to us in the rain. Fucking beautiful, man."

Echo and The Bunnymen 6/10

The drunk bloke with the shaved head and his top off staggers in front of me again. He holds his arms out and yells in my face as the rain splatters all over his head and mingles with the drink on his chin.

"Wot?" he says, looking straight at me, trying to be still, but not able to.

I don't say anything. My double jointed thumb twitches involuntarily.

Then he suddenly goes white and starts spitting and retching.

"He's gonna boke," says Russ. Russ told us the word. It's my favourite word right now. It's the sound you make when you retch and just stop yourself.

The drunk bloke walks off in no direction, bumping into people, spitting and retching, as boke-ready as anyone I've ever seen.

Half a song later he's back, drinking again.

"Let's go," says Catalina looking at him. It's before the end of the set.

Catalina once broke the nose of an ex-boyfriend. No one liked him.

Good Thai Dins

Good Thai Dins is punniest, but Catalina can't eat noodles because they remind her of worms. She finds a place she liked when she came the year before and we join the queue.

Spook has disappeared before. Two years ago he walked out of his job at the supermarket just after university and no one saw him again for eight months.

"You know when Spook went missing before...?" I say. I search for my inhaler. I have asthma. I have bad dreams about being in underground tunnels.

"What?" says Catalina, turning to Russ in his green waterproof.

"I've had my money nicked," he says. Russ goes red, proper, real red in the face.

I don't ask, because I already know how much it is.

Ambulance

"I heard they've found a couple of people dead in their tents over the years," says Catalina, her black bunches lank, drenched, and stuck to the side of her face, "but if you think how many people have come over how many years, that's not much, is it."

Then we step to the side to let the ambulance through, and we all think the same thing.

"He's ok," says Catalina, "he's just being Spook. He'll be fine." Catalina has a job in a post-production studio in London. She has responsibility. She can say things no one believes in a way that makes people sort of forget how much they don't believe them by.

Tom McRae 10/10

Catalina isn't feeling well so Russ takes her back to their tent. Russ can do first aid, he's got a certificate from work.
It's still raining. A few songs into the set the sun comes out like it means it.

Kiri had to work. She couldn't come with us. Kiri cooked me a meal last month for the first time. Then we laughed at things that weren't funny. I touched her arm to get her attention when I was talking and kept it there even when I'd run out of words. I think she noticed but she didn't move away.

She's set me three secret challenges. One is to sing the words to a song I like and pretend I'm singing to her.

When I stop singing the guy in front of me faints. I think it's from the heat. I only sang under my breath.

REM 8/10

"Tosh," I shout, enthusiastically, because I like this song. Secret challenge two is to shout out 'tosh' to a song and to get someone else to join in. Russ is with me. "Tosh," he says quietly at first, then shouts it out louder. Obviously I don't explain to him why he's shouting it.

Russ is posher than me. His grandfather was a millionaire, but gambled it all away. His grandfather is dead now.

Early Morning Saturday

Catalina has food poisoning. She has been boking and spewing since early morning. All the tents round us must have heard her. She looks as white as her free *Vodafone* groundsheet, her sick's as orange as the *Orange* poncho. She's sleeping now. There's a plastic bag shaped into a bowl by her head.

The ground is covered in a thick carpet of litter, cups, plastic bottles, polystyrene cartons, sections of the festival programme.

Russ reads the newspaper sitting cross-legged outside his tent. I am lying down thinking about Kiri, but I tell him I am just chilling.

t-shirts

My second favourite t-shirt, black, vibrating lettering on white: I AM VIBRATING AT THE SPEED OF LIGHT.

My first favourite t-shirt, pink bubble lettering on yellow: VAGINAS ARE WAY COOL.

Between bands, the Oxfam and Water Aid and look-after-the planet-it's-not-too-late-honest films play on the big screens on the Pyramid

Stage. A man with his family sit on sensible camping chairs. He has a *Shell Direct* t-shirt on.

A thing that happens

Russ goes to the tent to check on Catalina and get her to drink water. Russ can't face the chemical toilets. He says it mucks with his reading ritual.

Waiting for a band to come on at The Other Stage, a thing happens. It really happens. Other people see it too.

I wonder if this may be the most beautiful thing I've ever seen and I wonder what this says about me and how I live. I feel suddenly lonely that there's no one I know to share it. All my friends have never felt so far away. I have a sudden feeling that if I think about them hard enough when I'm looking they can see it too. Only a second or maybe two later I know I can't.

Feelings like this still surprise me, but I'm worried I'm learning how to deal with them quicker and see through them too soon. I don't want to know how to deal with them. I don't want to be able to see through them. I just want to have the feeling for keeping.

Flaming Lips 10/10

There are dancing people in animal suits and fake blood and giant colourful balloons pushed out into the crowd. Russ and I are near the front.

I jump up and hit a giant green balloon with the tips of my fingers and dedicate it to Kiri in a secret, no one ever needs to know kind of way, because this isn't the kind of thing you tell people anyway. Kiri smells so good sometimes I want all my body to just mash into hers.

Supergrass 9/10

"Are you ok, Russ?"

"Yeah," he says. But I don't believe him, his irony voice isn't working.

"Did you get a paper today?"

The band are just about to come on.

"No. Didn't feel like it. Can't concentrate."

Russ can speak fluent Spanish. I'm getting him a real Spanish newspaper for his birthday.

Radiohead 10/10

"I know," I say in a sudden idea kind of tone, to the guy who just pushed past in front of us. "Since you've only just got here and we've been here a while, maybe you could let my friend stand in front of you because you're so much taller than him – I just thought that was an idea and it would be nice of you."

He's very tall but he's pretty young and not muscley so I'm not really that worried. He looks down at me and pulls a face.

"But then I'd keep having to stand further back – I'd end up at the back."

The band play. People shout the words in my ears.

Walking back, there are just too many people. Just too many people.

Spook is ambidextrous. Spook can fly kites. I used to copy Spook's maths homework. I know how he got that cut over his eye and his mum doesn't. I know what songs he wants played if he's dead. I start listing them. I never know what Spook is thinking about.

I get a sudden feeling. If I can find my tent in the dark from all the thousands of others I can also find Spook from all the thousands of other people. Only I know I can't. I wish I'd packed a torch.

Early Morning Sunday

The tent next door to ours has been slashed. Everything inside is sodden.

Catalina is feeling better, but not full better. She has a craving for an orange. She says she wants a t-shirt saying: BOKE QUEEN.

Russ has constipation. We learn that Russ likes three poos a day, one in the morning, one before lunch, and one before he goes to sleep. We learn that Russ likes pooing. We learn that Catalina has been dreaming of pooing and is missing it. Usually she likes two poos a day. We also learn that I do not like talking about this as much as they do.

"Suit yerself," says Catalina. "Have you seen the size of Spook's poos?" I can't see her face. It's just a voice coming from her tent.

"No. Can we talk about something else now, please," I say, lying on my back in my tent.

"They're not big! They're really small…"

"Catalina!"

I am laughing though.

When Spook came back at the end of his eight months he was wearing sandals and a dressing gown. His mum said he knocked on the door, said hi, walked in, said he was tired, went to bed, got up eight hours later, had a bath, ate breakfast and started talking as if nothing had happened, asking after the family and the pets and asking if she needed anything when he went into town to get a job.

Sub-letting

I go for a walk and find an area just off the main path up the hill from the Pyramid Stage and it's all fenced off in blue plastic lattice-work tape. There's a sign by a tent saying room for rent. £40 a night.

The third challenge is to bring Kiri something back. Kiri broke her leg once. She's got a metal bar in it. She says she goes off in airports. I've touched the scar. I like how it's there but didn't know how to say so without it coming out wrong. We never talk about her boyfriend.

There are too many shops and I don't like it so I don't want to buy anything. I consider stealing something, but can't think of anything Kiri might actually want. I walk past the shops and think about how good it would be if there wasn't anything at all to bring back, if there weren't any shops at all.

Damien Rice 10/10

Catalina and Russ are both out.

"You know when Spook went missing before?" I say, and I can feel Catalina looking at me already.

"What about it?" she says.

"Did he ever speak to you, because he's never told me anything."

She doesn't reply. For a moment I think she's not going to and is waiting for the band to start so we can't talk anymore.

"All he said was about getting his head straight."

I nod.

"See, that's all he said to me."

Russ looks back at Catalina.

"So if he came back does that mean he got it sorted?" I ask.

Men with bags of beer walk among the crowd charging exorbitant prices.

Beth Gibbons 10/10

"It's like she's a little embarrassed girl," says Russ, "then she starts a song and she's suddenly this mysterious portal and channel for all the world's sorrow."

By now people around us are starting to smell and we wonder how much we smell as well.

The Streets 5/10

"It's the sound," I say, "I can't hear anything apart from the bass – maybe it's ok if you're in the middle."

Russ trips over something as we pile out of the tent. He puts his hands out to stop himself.

"Hello, Spook," says Catalina, calm as sitcom cool, "what you doing on the ground?"

"Dunno," he says. "Relaxing." He's only wearing a pair of shorts he doesn't own and some enormous shades. His skin is silver with rainwater. No one says anything, not even Russ. We just stare. Spook is tapping his feet to the bassline.

On the train on the way back

We get up at 5am to get away from the crush of people. We take a train to Bristol – most people are going East so we get rid of them quicker this way.

"So, then," says Russ, "favourite bits and disappointments?" I'm looking out of the window thinking about the bath I'm going to have.

"I like the anticipation of the whole thing," says Catalina, her black hair in a ponytail.

"And the worst bit?" says Russ.

"I think you can probably guess," she says. "You?"

"My worst bit was the loos," he says slowly, "my favourite bit was Radiohead."

"My worst bit was the crowds," I say. "There were just too many people…or maybe how it was just…you know, just a music festival, it wasn't anything more than that, was it?"

"Howdyoumean?" says Russ, scrunching up his face, leaning forwards.

"I just mean…" I don't know why, but I look over to Spook, as if he is going to help me. He looks out of the window and doesn't turn round.

"I just mean, we didn't stop a war or find a new way to live or anything like that, did we."

Russ looks at Catalina, and she looks back at him.

"No," says Russ, shrugging his shoulders.

"But, on the flipside of that," I say, "my favourite bit was the dancing animals and the giant balloons."

"Spook?" says Russ.

"What?"

"Favourite bit and worst bit?"

Spook looks confused for a moment.

"Favourite bit was the whole thing, just everything about it, everything – and the worst bit is leaving."

Spook looks back out of the window, so does everyone else.

"I really did like the dancing animals and the giant balloons," I say, almost taking myself by surprise, "but I think my real favourite bit wasn't that."

So I try to explain what I saw and even Spook looks at me when I'm talking. I try and tell them just exactly how it was. I haven't forgotten any of it.

In the heat the wind whipped up into a mini vortex, picking the litter up off the ground, whipping it round and round like a whirlpool in the sky, slapping the tents as it picked up speed, getting higher and higher, as high as the birds. When you looked up and watched as it drifted higher you really couldn't tell the difference between the rubbish, the plastic bags, the scraps of paper and the crisp packets, from the birds flying directly overhead with their glitteringly white wings flashing high up in the clearest blue of the sky, so high you couldn't keep looking because your eyes started to water with all that light.

14 Everyday Brands

1. Next

Their affordable styling in Tailored Suits, Smart Casual shirts and Formal Shoes meet my needs as a young professional who can't afford not to look good in the office.

I also favour these ranges for interviews. There are other jobs out there, but I'll only jump ship when the right opportunity comes up.

They do a range of Gadgets and Gifts too. I have some football pitch cufflinks. There are tiny balls in them and you can try and score goals waiting for meetings to start.

Their Smart Casual, Casualwear, Eveningwear, and Footwear ranges are also favourites of my girlfriend, Emma. Their Lingerie and Nightwear range is a joint favourite. We have been together 7 years. I'm told it's normal; after a while you start dressing pretty much the same as each other.

2. John Smith's Bitter

An unpretentious, solid workaday beer for those mid-week drinks with my friend Carl. He says 'the Stuck Feeling is normal'. He says he has it sometimes. He has thrown himself into DIY. He says I should throw myself into something. I have decided to throw myself into the house and domestic life.

3. Tesco

Weekend shopping in the biggest store we can find. We shop as a team. She is in control of the trolley, like the aircraft carrier at the centre of the fleet making its way through the aisles. I am the marine commando party sent out for raid missions. Our cupboards will be full.

4. Aerial

We have had no problems with the stains and smells from our clothes. We can go back to work on Mondays smelling and looking good.

5. De Cecco

Quality olive oil for the young professional couple serious about learning to cook.

6. Cif

This makes the house clean for our guests. Our friends come and stay the night, and they bring their babies and the bathroom is clean. Sometimes Emma and I talk about having kids.

7. Fairy

We use lashings of this for our dinner parties.

8. Finish

A dishwasher seemed the logical step if we were going to have this many dinner parties.

9. Listerene

Our dinner parties are getting more experimental and the food richer.

10. Coca Cola

Our friends' kids are growing up. We have this in for them. Sometimes it's quite refreshing if the cans are kept in the fridge.

11. Colgate

Essential to keep those teeth into the next week after refreshing cans of soft drinks kept in fridge.

12. Grolsch

A stronger lager for those weekend blow-outs with my friend Tom. I have told him that I am thinking of leaving Emma. He has told me this would be a serious mistake and I would regret it. He says I should change my job or move house instead. He has suggested joining a gym with him.

13. Reebok

We have joined a gym. We go twice a week after work. I have been for a couple of interviews but the jobs weren't right and I didn't get offered them anyway. I can't think of anywhere else I especially would like to live, and I need to be near here if I still work where I do.

14. North Face

I have left Emma. I have taken up hill walking. I go every other weekend with Tom. I now feel less stuck. He was right, I do regret it.

Theory of Accidents

1: Jane Lies About Her Name

I am not a reliable witness because I don't always tell the truth. If I never told the truth I'd actually be more reliable, not less.

On this particular occasion I was coming out of the village shop with a bag in each hand, which has its pluses and minuses – I like to be balanced up, but then I can easily start imagining itches into existence all over parts of my face. I remember a man with a moustache and his glasses on a chain hung round his neck – over a comfy dad style golf jumper – held the door open for me on the way out. It was one of those bright winter days when the sun is so sharp it's like it's slanting in from under its usual position, beneath where the clouds were expecting it to be, so they can't work out how to stop it: like it was actually far brighter and whiter than when it was summer. There was no one else walking on the pavement – it's the main road in the village – goes right through it – it's a 30 zone. There were cars parked up on both sides of the road like usual. The sun was hitting their roofs and windscreens, sort of turning the light metal. I was walking away from the sun at this point (or was I?) so it felt all warm and large on my back and I started thinking of the exact spot in my garden where I could stand to get just the same feel when I got back home. (If I even lived in that village.)

A little further up the street on the opposite side to me, two guys in blue denim jackets got into a black BMW Z3 – the ones that look like angry souped-up giant metal slippers. The guys had the clichéd clean cut good looks masking conventional bad thoughts of a conveyor belt boy band kind – which is rare in the village; as rare as cars like theirs.

They fired up the engine, with its straining to be a boy racer exhaust, and I was almost up level with them. As I put one bag down to scratch a non-existent itch on my nose, from behind came a rumble, zoom, crash and a vroom. A clean-me white Peugeot 306 with three people in it shattered the wing mirror of the BMW and didn't stop. The glass from the wing mirror splayed out slow motion across the road, catching the sun, sowing out like diamonds, glinting jagged edges. You know when you get those sun stars on the surface of water – it was like that but on the road. If you squinted both eyes you could push all the other detail away and just see the tiny stings of light twinkling back up at you.

One of the boy band people got out, swearing like a footballer, picked up the wing mirror, got back in, slammed the door, and the pair of them screeched off in the direction of the Peugeot.

I scooped up a few pieces and put them in my coat pocket.

When I put them on the kitchen table my boyfriend (if I had one) said:

"Janey, where'd you get all that?"

"Don't call me that," I said, "I was on my way to market with our cow when a guy offered me these instead."

"If you're in one of these moods I'm going to meet Pete and Rich down the pub," and he put on his coat and left.

I put the shopping away and decided I definitely had to go back and live in a town. Unless you're born there, you shouldn't try and live in the country unless you're old, or you feel contented.

The bits of mirror looked better where they'd been, and I mostly wished I'd just left them there.

2: Gavin and Lina Have A Plan

One of our favourite places to go at the time was just outside a village where Lina's Gran used to live; it looked like somewhere in a magazine, but was better because it wasn't in one. We were going to go for a drive – get Lina – as in Angelina – out of her parents' house for a bit, and me out of my parents' house. I'd borrowed my mum's car specially, and the day had started with a sun that seemed to mean business.

But pretty soon we realised we didn't want to go to that village today, we fancied somewhere else for a change, but neither of us could even think of a place to head for. We'd driven 3.6 miles out of town when it started to rain – I always zeroed the milometer when I borrowed my parents' cars, out of habit I think, or maybe just in case anything ever happened and I wanted to know how far I'd driven if it ever did.

"3.6," I said, though I thought it was to myself.

"What?" said Lina.

"Nothing."

1.4 miles later we decided to pull over in the space of a gateway just off the road. Pretty much just as we pulled in was the first time the radio played Britney and *Toxic*. Lina switched to another station almost straight away, to find Bowie singing *Heroes*.

The rain pelleted into the windscreen in tiny definite thuds and the sound made me more aware of the difference between inside the car and outside. It gave me a goldfish feeling as we sat in the car listening to the rain and David Bowie barely able to see anything as the mist came down and smeared a grey flannel over everywhere we looked. In front was the line of hedges bordering the whole road. Through the rear windscreen I couldn't see beyond the 'Strictly No Admittance' sign, its white lettering over a red background hanging on the wooden gate.

"Gav, what are you doing with your mouth?"

"Nothing," I said, taken by surprise, some place miles away in my own thoughts.

"With your cheeks then – you were puffing them out then making your mouth gape open."

"No I wasn't," I said. Then Britney came on again. I went to change it.

"No, leave it," she said. "Let's listen to it."

So we listened to it, feeling that familiar blend of superiority over pop music in its risible lyrics and highly marketable shallowness running simultaneously with an inferiority at its pervasiveness, feeling threatened and defeated by how it defined our times far more than we did ourselves – and since we were the ones who chose to buy it, or not, and not the other way round, that never seemed right.

"Ok?" I said as the DJ spoke all over the strings at the end that I actually quite liked.

"Yep – but if it comes on again we're leaving."

After that we started talking about our Plan. Our Plan was to move abroad and start up a language school. We seemed to work all the time and moan about stress and not sleeping and what with house prices the way they are we couldn't afford anywhere remotely near where we worked anyway.

I did Italian at university and Lina's dad is Italian and she's spent a third of her life there. We'd teach English to locals and get people from England over, put them in her Other Gran's old cottage – do it up so it was nice, and teach them Italian.

We'd been working on getting the money together for our Plan for the last eight months. We were both working as teachers, living with our parents and taking on any extra marking work for extra money whenever we could. The coming summer we'd go out there and start making enquiries and trying to find the best place for the classes. A friend of mine from university was going to help us get our website sorted in time for Christmas. The Plan was, the summer after this one coming we'd leave work, head out there, and start our Actual Proper Lives.

A Ronan Keating song came on which we'd already heard that day. Lina turned it over. Atomic Kitten. A moment of indecision, then onto another channel where Pink wanted the party started.

There were still a load of details to sort out. I don't think either of us really believed that actually it was ever really going to happen. That was partly what we were hoping our trip out this year would help clear up. Lina's dad was going to help us with some of the money, but we still needed to find almost half of it from somewhere else and it felt like neither of us was going to admit to the other that chickens even existed let alone admitting whether they ever laid eggs or not. Still, we just sort of liked talking about it because that way it was as if we weren't neglecting it – as if the Plan was so fragile it might not make it from week to week unless we constantly looked after it – helped it grow up from theory to practice.

The opening strings of *Toxic* came on for the third time that afternoon and Lina turned it up loud, put her hands over her ears, and yelled: 'go.'

So we did. We hadn't seen a single car or bike in the whole time we'd been waiting. Now, just as we wanted to leave, a dirty white car in the road – with what looked like three passengers inside – stopped and flashed its lights at us to let us pull out in front of it. In my central mirror it looked like it pulled into the gateway just behind us, then I lost sight of it.

We drove off into the mist and the rain, and it was hard to see that clearly where we were going and neither of us had any real idea where we were heading for all over again.

3: Strictly No Admittance

The four of us were out for a bike ride, which, in spite of the clear summer sky and light breeze, was a big mistake. Stuart – friend I'm always going to have no matter what, because of everything – his boyfriend, Brian – selfish, self-centred, Stuart-obsessed, manipulative, drama empress, camp beyond camp and all levels of campness fake, must do something remarkable in bed because I have no idea why Stuart is with him – though Stuart says it's just Brian's insecurity and when he's more relaxed I'll understand – Markmark, my boyfriend – serious?/not serious?, not sure – and me, Zadie – trying real hard to get on with Brian. Who is a cunt.

At the top of the hill, Brian: "I soooo have to stop or I'll die right now! I think it's broken. Did anyone see it? Did anyone see me?"

"Stop it" said Markmark.

"I didn't say anything."

"Let's stop here for a bit then," said Stuart. I caught his look and he couldn't hide it from me. Brian, in all the kit, found a way of getting off a bike that was part swoon, part delicacy and all watch me watch me. He carried the limp in his leg from his fall as if the small red graze on his knee was a probable fracture – he looked up to see if we were watching so he could gauge how much effort to put into his limp. We all pretended we hadn't seen him and the four of us collected by two large metal gridded doors with a full on summer tree giving off Big Green either side.

"How about we break here for lunch?" suggested Markmark, cheery tone in his voice.

"I don't eat lunch," said Brian, laying on his back now, his arms over the top of his face.

"Can this be your tea then? Have it early," said Markmark.

"I don't eat lunch," said Brian, quieter.

I glugged back some water from my plastic water bottle and handed it out.

"Water?"

A Markmark acceptance, a Stuart refusal.

"What's that then?" said Brian, snatching a look at my A to E marks on my arm. I'm normally so careful about that. In the heat I'd pushed up my sleeve and forgotten to push it down again. I pushed it down now in two quick strikes of my hand.

"Drink some water, Brian, you're thirsty," said Stuart.

"Well, I'm thinking of having a snack at least," said Markmark.

I saw Stuart reading the sign on the metal doors at the same time as me.

"Strictly No Admittance."

"No," said Markmark.

Strictly No Admittance signs are too much to resist. They are my favoured leisure activity.

I found a way up a tree as Markmark started saying sensible things and Brian started saying, "Stus don't you dare follow her, don't you dare."

"Course he's going – he's just as stupid as her," said Markmark.

"Leave him out of this," said Brian, "he's not!"

There was a pretty easy route up the branches and then you just dropped down the other side of the gate.

"Stus, I really don't think you should be doing that!"

Only Stuart followed, landing seconds after I'd rolled clear on almost the exact same patch of colour drained yellow grass.

"Stus! Stus! Stus!"

"And how you going to get back?" said Markmark.

I snapped a few quick looks around me and wondered the same thing.

"Markmark," I said, "if you're going to just say sensible things all day at least say them before they're too late."

"Stus, you ok? Stus, are you hurt?"

So the two of us followed the path between the hedges and went to see what we were Strictly Not Admitted to.

"You know what I think it is?" said Stuart, as we followed the path down a slope and the hedges either side started to fall away, before we got our first glimpses of what was in the hollow of the valley.

"I agree," I said. I'd smelt it too.

So we didn't say anything else, just walked to the corner. Then we stood there and looked at the valley of large open concrete circles that made up the wide open view of the sewage treatment works.

4: Saturdaze

Saturdaze: to induce a state of being dazed or a stupor brought on as a result of over-saturation in Saturday morning television mostly consisting of pre-football match chat and analysis and entertainment world and pop music news, interviews and current hits.

5: Morning Selves and Evening Selves

Zadie and I hadn't broken up much before and, since it was amicable enough, she still let me use her car during the week because I needed it for work till I got my own, and she could use the bus. That's why I still had a set of keys. I would have asked, but since it was a thing to do with Tab I thought Zade wouldn't want to know, and there was no need for her to know, and anyway, I'd put back what I took before she even knew it had gone. Only I didn't.

I left a note by Tab's front door to find in the morning reminding me to put back what I'd taken from Zadie's car. Morning Selves are slower and need the help of Evening Selves to get things done. But Morning Selves are fuller of good intentions and Evening Selves take advantage of them. The midday and afternoon respect between them is my most productive time, but at either end of the day accusations are rife, language is colourful in the morning, and thoughts are plotting and manipulate at night.

The note fell down the back of the radiator – blew down in the draft from the way Tab shuts the door, no doubt. So I forgot to put back what I'd taken and two days later Zadie rang up to be angry about it.

The radiator has since maintained a reticent plea of innocence throughout, which neither Morning or Evening Self have built a convincing case against, but the afternoon brought a compromise in which they both decided to blame it anyway, and to cover all bases by asking Tab to close her front door with less whoosh in future. I asked her in the evening and fucking off was the option she gave me – not that an actual alternative was given. Knowing this to be her Evening Self, and therefore not a fully considered collective response on the matter I decided to get my Morning Self to ask her again in the morning, but to do it rather more brightly and cheerily than before.

On doing so, her Morning Self was very much of the opinion that: 1. it was her door and she would shut it in the manner of her own choosing, 2. my options were to be fucking off, or to have no options, and 3. that on this morning the chosen style of door shutting was very much inclined to the whoosh.

So it was that I forgot what I was supposed to remember and it was left by the side of the bed in Tab's place where we'd slipped strips of paper into it, making notes for our trip up to Killin in Scotland – or Scotlandshire in England as it is now, after we happened to over-hear an American tourist call it that.

6. Travelling in Space and Time

I was looking down the back of the boiler for another blue sock to go with the one I'd already found. My mum always said blue socks were a Zadie trademark. Instead of the one I wanted I found the green one of Markmark's I'd been looking for a couple of months earlier, around the time when we were splitting up. He'd gone to one of the pubs we used to go to with Anna and Chris to watch the football one Saturday, but I didn't fancy it – went to Stuart's instead and painted his kitchen. At the pub Markmark bumped into Tabitha, who he used to know at university but hadn't seen for four years since they left – the story goes they knocked into each other, spilt beers on each other and started talking. I don't really know the details, and actually don't want to know, except that it sounds as if Markmark was in two places at once on more than a few occasions in that time.

Six weeks later he was moving out and I was putting up a card for a lodger in the Londis shop window. Markmark agreed to pay rent till the end of the lease, or until I got someone in, whichever happened first.

I've seen pictures of Tabitha.

On this particular morning – this morning when I found Markmark's green sock instead of my blue sock – I had decided I wanted to go somewhere and do something, so, not wanting to lose the moment, I cut my losses, put Markmark's sock on and not more than two morning songs on the radio later was out of the flat walking towards my car.

This was a fantastic and encouraging performance by a Morning Me, to use Markmark's theory, I have always preferred Morning Mes to Evening ones, especially when the sun's out. Evening Mes can be so somber. At least it generally knows when it's like that to keep itself to itself.

The night before it was watching the news about the body of a missing girl being found. It was thinking: what about the people who don't even make it to the news? What about the people they don't ever find? What about the people from history no one even knows the names of? If just one person is missing the whole thing is ruined. When my sister Abbie was made to disappear she was 17. She would be 21 now. She got a mention in the local newspaper. The column was 8mm from top to bottom and 28mm across.

My car is the first and only I have ever bought. I used the money my gran left me to buy it secondhand. I have washed it twice since then. That was nearly three years ago. I will clean it soon. Next week maybe. I usually clean it next week. It's a Peugeot 306 and it is supposed to be white. The longer I leave between cleans the more astounding it will look to me when it does get cleaned. Last time I cleaned it, it looked so zingy and white it looked white enough for angels to borrow it – I would've let them too if they'd asked – I wouldn't even have minded taking the bus to work if that was the reason – some indication of when they'd return it would have been appreciated though. Just imagine how white it would look if I left it for a few more years; or imagine leaving it for millions of years, then being found by future people who cleaned it up. It would be like their equivalent of the Arc of the Covenant or something – plus being white it would not only be inherently fashionable – because white goes with everything – but it would also really suit the future because white is always used in sci-fi for spaceships and all kinds of things.

Only my car did need cleaning, so it looked just like an ordinary dirty car with scum and muck all over its once white paint – which, right then, is exactly what it was.

I unlocked it and got in. I put the key in the ignition, checked my mirrors and seatbelted up. At that point I had no way of knowing that Markmark had taken anything.

On the drive I started thinking of my brother and about how I ought to give him a text to say hello. He's quite a bit younger than me and at nine he asked me to explain my physics degree to him. I was explaining how worm holes are where black holes meet, they're places where you can, theoretically, travel through time and space. A black hole, a collapsed star, is like a tear in space-time. Instead of thinking of space and time as two separate things, think of them as the same thing – like a stretchy sheet of rubber – you put something on it and it sinks a little in the sheet, put something with more mass – so it has more gravity – and it sinks even lower into the sheet. Put something with so much gravity – like a black hole – which has so much gravity in it not even light can escape from it – and you end up tearing the sheet. The joins between two tears or more are worm holes. If you stood just outside a black hole and put one leg in it would stretch on and on through the black hole, stretched out into spaghetti. If that black hole is also a worm hole and a worm hole exists just above your head the end of your foot could come down and rest on your head, so that way you could really be in two places at once.

"Oh, yeah," he said, his eyes widening and sparkling, like he really had got it, "that explains how socks disappear."

So my brother, at the age of nine proved the existence of worm holes in a little under five minutes, then went out to head a football against a wall.

I thought he'd forgotten all about it, but a week later he woke me up real early one morning and shook my shoulder and asked if Abbie would use worm holes to come back and would it be ok if he kept worms in the house to help them just in case?

7: Albumming

Ringing the buzzer I already had a pretty good idea of how I'd find them, so I was expecting a wait for the door to open. I was pretty sure I'd find them already pretty Saturdazed into semi-comas, both with tracksuit trousers and vests on with bare feet, both unshaven with scruffy morning hair. No answer, so I rang Stuart's mobile.

"Cup of coffee?" said Stuart, squinting slightly from the daylight and stepping away to let me in, his mobile in one hand, still on and beeping at him because I'd cleared.

"I'll make it," I said. "You two get ready, because we're going out."

"Are we?" said Stuart, not with it.

"Hello Zade," said Brian, also wearing tracksuit trousers, a vest and no socks, running his hands through what existed of his short cropped morning hair.

"Hey Bri, you ok?"

"Yeah, sure, good to see you...what we doing?"

"We're going for a drive."

"Oh," he said, and stood rubbing his arm, in an absent sort of way, as he watched Stuart head off to the bedroom.

"What?"

"It's just we were watching...the...there's the new Kylie vid coming up and..."

"We've seen it!" shouted Stuart from the other room.

"Not the beginning!" said Brian, looking at me, with sort of pleading eyes.

I didn't need to say anything.

"Stus, where's my sleeveless puffer!" he called into the bedroom as he walked towards it.

It was Stuart who came up with saturdazing, he came up with mondead too, for when you feel like a zombie all day on a Monday and don't want to do anything in the evening so you go back home and have an early night.

Stuart came up with Undercover Agents when we were at school. At lunchtime the idea was to go into furniture showrooms, and without being kicked out, get into a bed, actually get inside the covers if there were any, and lie there for a minute – we'd take it in turns to be undercover or be on stopwatch duty. Off the back of that I came up with Narnia – in which you had to hide in a wardrobe, then the decoy man would lead an unsuspecting sales assistant towards the wardrobes, then the Narnian would leap out, the assistant would freak, usually swear, and we'd both leggit. Soon there weren't any places left in our town we were allowed in so we had to think of something new.

That was when Stuart came up with Albumming. The idea was to get a free listen of an entire album, but there were tricky rules. You had to ask for the same album from the same sales person in the same shop each time, and you had to ask at least three different times, all in the same week. Over the course of a few weeks this soon turned into the Albummer getting extra kudos if they dressed up differently on each occasion, successfully hiding their identity right the way through. Our best effort ever was when we sorta borrowed the panto horse they were using at school for the end of year review thing, took it out in the lunchtime, got into it, clip-clopped into HMV and listened to two different albums on two different headphones (I was the bum end) without ever getting out of the costume. We were spotted by the French teacher as we were galloping back to the store cupboard at school. But through natural skill we were able to dump it off and get through a window before we were caught – and since the teacher only saw the horse, not us, no one ever knew who it was. Half of the school claimed it was them at one time or another. We stopped Albumming after that coz we knew it couldn't get any better.

8: Precision Sleeping

"So where did you say we were going?" said Stuart, sitting in the front passenger seat.

"I didn't."

"Loosey goosey Stus," said Brian from the back seat as we waited for the lights to amber out of red.

"Loosey goosey," I agreed.

I was gonna take them all to a pub in the country I went to years ago with my dad where they did good lunches, but of course, that didn't happen, because of the thing I'm about to tell you that happened instead.

Stuart was car DJ and rifled through CDs, most of which he'd given me at one time or another, unless they were the ones I'd borrowed but never returned. As we took the exit at the roundabout for the dual carriageway we headed in the direction of the low winter sun, just as one large raincoat grey cloud stepped out in front of it to flash its mac in the sun's face.

"Take it we're eating inside?" said Stuart, deadpan.

"Like a goose," said flat Brian. "Be loose as a goose. My friend."

We took the turning off at the first exit and that led us to a roundabout, then a main road, then a right turn off that and we were on a proper country road, with hedges either side.

"Hey Stus, Zade, I couldn't sleep last night, and you wanna know what I was thinking while the rhino here was being the zee keeper?"

"What?" said Stuart, not taking offence at his rhinoship, "what were you thinking?"

"See, I was wondering what was going on in the rhino's head, and if he was dreaming right then or not, and then I was thinking about how amazing it would be if you could be in other people's dreams and if they could be in yours, just swap between them when you were sleeping, and I was wondering if the people in my dreams were always there because I made them be there, or if, actually, maybe they'd made themselves be there…"

I came to a junction, couldn't be sure which way to go, and decided to avoid the village the sign was pointing towards and keep going. I remembered something about the village being the wrong way to go – though not which village that actually was.

"…so what I was thinking was maybe if you fell asleep at exactly, I mean *exactly* the same time, same *split split* second, as someone else, no matter where they were at the time, no matter how far away you were from them, then that meant you could travel freely between each other's dreams till you woke up."

"Yeah, I see," said Stuart, "sort of precision sleeping."

I can't believe I ever didn't like Brian.

9: My First Car Chase

As we stopped at a T-junction which I thought I recognised, in my central mirror I saw a car accelerating right up behind us, flashing its lights and sounding its horn. I had a bunny in headlights moment and just froze as I watched it, shiny and black with its front grill grinning like evil teeth. It didn't look like it was going to stop. Bits of my brain found time to think of *Knight Rider*, the film *Duel* and Darth Vader's mouth.

"What?" said Stuart, and I realised what was happening.

Two guys in blue denim jumped out of the car, and in no time there was one either side of our car, thumping at the windows with the flats of their fists.

"Go!" shouted Stuart.

"Wankers!" shouted Brian, and I lurched the car away, not looking back.

I was changing gear without being able to hear them because my heart was hammering away so loud my whole body felt sound-proofed – letting nothing in, but nothing out either.

In my mirrors I could see the insecty black car catching up.

"Down there!" shouted Stuart, and I turned where he said, barely braking, skidding on the gravel but righting the car quick, just getting it into a right hand corner in time.

"There's three of us," shouted Brian.

"What if they've got weapons, Bri?" shouted Stuart.

"Then we'll get weapons!" he shouted back.

The road was full of bends and seemed to be getting narrower, I kept accelerating with a feeling that we were bound to run straight into a car coming the other way.

"I'm going to ram them!" I shouted, still driving away from them as fast as I could. The teeth of their car appeared in my mirror as they were catching up through the bends in the road.

"They get out and I'm going to reverse right into them!" I shouted, as the bends seemed to be getting tighter – the hedges so dense on either side you couldn't tell how the road was going or if cars were heading for us.

"Left!" shouted Stuart, and at another tight T-junction I swung the car into a sharp corner and kept going, missing a gear in the panic before I found one again. The revs started to climb like someone scrambling up a ladder that was getting narrower and narrower.

The hedges wiped past me on either side as the road straightened out and the car wouldn't go any faster. The sound of the high revs started to sink into the background, like a fan I couldn't remember turning on or off.

And some time went.

"Hey!" said Stuart, but I don't know when.

"Hey!" he said, and I realised I could hear ok.

"I think we're ok now, I get to say we lost them – you can say it too if you like."

Nothing in the mirrors, just a constant no black car behind us sight, blink after blink.

He rubbed my hand on the steering wheel nearest him. I looked at my hand and was struck by how white my knuckles were.

I lifted my foot a little from the accelerator, glancing at it, surprised to feel it so far down, with the peddle touching the floor of the car, catching a glimpse of Markmark's green sock as I did.

No one spoke, as the atmosphere inside the car tried to right itself.

At the next signpost I didn't recognise any of the places.

"Where are we?" I asked, sort of to no one, and no one answered.

"Maybe we could turn around and go home," I said. "Stuart, get the map out," and pointed under his seat, then took the chance to see the grooves of the steering wheel pattern in the palms of my hands and to feel them, like the insides of two griddle pans rubbing against each other.

Stuart ran his hands under the seat, then took his belt off to reach further. Brian reached under from the back.

"No map, Zade," said Stuart.

"Markmark!" I shouted and slapped the steering wheels with my hands.

Not long after that I was going to wish we'd just kept on going no matter where, because stopping seemed about the most stupid thing I could have done. And stopping is what I did.

10: Not Long After That

We parked up on the main road of the first village we found – seemed like the only road, it just ran right through it. As we did, the first tiny soundless drops of rain appeared on the windscreen, coming all together, like a transparent sheet with tiny bobbles on it being placed there.

We were totally lost. Our plan was to ask directions in the shop. All three of us got out, we started on Brian, volunteering him for asking duties. But he only agreed if he went in on his own – he didn't want his technique being overheard and ridiculed.

Waiting outside under the canopy as it started to ping and splat with bigger raindrops, we saw a girl about our age, who dressed more city than country, on the other side of the road. She sprinkled something onto the road, stood back on the pavement and looked at it for a bit, just standing in the rain without a coat on, then walked back in the direction she'd come from.

Stuart looked at me. When she was far enough away we stepped out into the rain and crossed over the road to see what she'd been doing. Looked like bits of broken mirror.

Brian came out of the shop with a plastic carrier bag in each hand.

"I got lunch!" he shouted to us on the other side of the road.

"Directions?" I said as we got nearer.

"Ah," he said, with his I knew there was something face.

"You're joking!" said Stuart, exasperated.

"Yep," said Brian, and walked on towards the car.

We decided to find somewhere for lunch, even though we weren't all that sure where we were going. I didn't actually feel at all like eating, and the rain was turning from swarm of insects style – fast busy and light – to full on power shower style – if you had soap with you you really could shower in it. When I stayed with Stuart at his aunt's house in the Cotswold's that summer it rained like this. Stuart's aunt has a large garden and no immediate neighbours. We took the shower gel with us and showered in it, so I know I'm right.

I'd started to get so used to the windscreen wiper sound I didn't really notice it anymore. I'd started to time the thoughts in my head with them, so the emphasis bits would fall at the end of the down wipe.

"Shall we just find a place to park?" said Stuart.

"Eat it in the car?" said Brian. "Yeah – wot you reckon, Zade?"

"Sure, if…we see…anywhere." For the past two miles all we'd seen were hedgerows, one turning off the main road – which I didn't want to take in case I lost my bearings – and one gateway.

"Why you talking…like a…robot, Zade?" said Brian.

"What about just up here?" said Stuart.

"Looks like…there's someone…there," I said.

"Think they're leaving," he said.

I flashed my lights to let them, and there was a small green VW with a couple in it. I was sure I could hear Britney giving it *Toxic* from the speakers of their car till they turned it down.

"Here, then?" I said.

"Why not?" said Stuart, so I drove forward, then reversed back into the gateway.

Stuart put a CD on and we tucked into our Brian-bought lunch.

On the second song the rain slowed up. On the third song it stopped and the sky suddenly felt cleaner and brighter than ever before in the way it sometimes does straight after rain.

I saw it on the fourth song.

On the fifth song Stuart wound his window down. He reached out and adjusted the direction of the wing mirror.

"How long you seen that?" he said.

"While ago," I said.

"What?" said Brian.

I pointed past him, through the back windscreen.

"Ah, I see," he said. "Can I finish this apple before we go?" he said.

"That's not up to me," I said.

I turned back round and the sun was starting to reflect off the *Strictly No Admittance* sign, making it hard to read if I sat back in a comfy position in my seat.

Then I sat forward and snapped the CD off.

"What?" said Stuart.

This was when I wished we'd just kept on going no matter where, because stopping seemed about the most stupid thing I could have done. They'd found us.

"There's a car," I said. My voice seemed to come from somewhere right in the pit of my stomach.

It was a car engine, somewhere along the road, getting closer. I was listening so hard it felt like I was turning into just a pair of ears

My hand went to the ignition key and my fingers clasped round it, ready to turn, and I felt like I was turning into just a finger and thumb.

Then I knew it would be coming round the bend any second and I turned into just a pair of eyes.

A dirty off-white Peugeot 306 – just like mine – with three passengers drove past in front of us.

11: The Ground That Wasn't There

Stuart jumped over the wooden gate first, followed by me, then Brian.

We landed one after the other, on the mud patch either side of the worn out grass.

"What do you think it is?" said Brian.

"Oh, you must never say!" I explained.

"But can you think about it?"

"Oh, no, that's even worse – you just have to get what you're given."

The path started to lead us uphill. Trees either side were spindly and leafless. There was a smell of rain and soil, but it wasn't as dark and deep a smell as I was expecting it to be.

The backs of my calves started to pull and my feet slipped in a shallow mud as the hill started to bite. Stuart and Brian were up ahead when I lost my balance and made an 'aaah' throat noise as I lunged for the dark trunk of a tree to stop me falling back. I missed most of the trunk, just scraping some wet bark into my fingernails, got a few strands of a branch, which slipped through my fingers and snapped back and whacked me onto the mud, where I was going anyway. The others heard it and skidded down the mud slope towards me. They asked me to give them a proper warning if I was going to do something as dramatic as that again, because they'd missed most it.

"You should pay more attention then, you never can tell what's going to happen around me," I said as they pulled me up, taking one of my hands in each of their two and heaving.

"And yer not getting in my car like that!" said Stuart.

"Which is my car." I pointed out.

"You know the point I'm making." And I did.

"It'll dry," I said, and they both repeated it, one after the other, as if that sort of helped. We started up the hill again; in front of us trees either side and a white sign too far away for us to read.

"What about this, then?" Brian had found a metal gate leading off the path to the left. It looked narrower and darker and much less of a path at all, but the old white sign with black writing to one side of the gate already meant that was the only way for us: *No Admittance To Public.*

Stuart went on ahead, through the trees, dull semi-muted snaps of twigs and forest ground things as he went, and the lie of the land was starting to dip down away from us now, the toes of my boots starting to slam into their ends and crumple up, like little bags of bones all mashed up.

"Does this ground feel firm to you?" I said to Brian who was next to me at the time, as I sprung up and down on it with the heel of a boot.

"Stu, wait up a sec!" I called.

And right then is when, through the mesh of winter trees in our line of sight, we saw Stu drop away as if the ground had just opened up. Brian later said he heard him make a 'waaah' sound as he went, but I don't remember that. I just remember the way he dropped, and the silence as there was no sound of him landing anywhere.

12: A to J

Abbie was walking out of school with her friends when she turned her foot on a kerb and broke the heel off her shoe. She said her foot was ok but said she was going back to her locker to change into another pair of shoes. Her friends all offered to come back with her, but she said no and told them to get on the bus – it would be there any moment. She said there was no reason for them to miss it too, and she'd catch the next one.

After the police were called they opened her locker and found her broken shoes in there, so they know she went back. But no one knows for sure what happened after that, though everyone I know has their own thoughts on that and keeps them to themselves.

None of the bus drivers remember seeing her. At seventeen she was used to getting buses on her own. They found her notebook, with a list of things to do and a list of things she had coming up.

When Stuart came to stay in my room in halls two weeks later, I knew he noticed the first letter on my arm one morning, but didn't say anything.

Six months later, two days after the body the police had found that turned out not to be Abbie's I was in Stuart's flat for the night, trying to be asleep. Stuart said he knew I wasn't asleep.

"Tell me about your arms," he said.

"No," I said, "I don't think I will," but then I surprised myself and suddenly changed my mind.

"We used to…" and it was too late to change it back.

"We used to cover the whole alphabet, when we were little, before Kieron was born, I used to think how we covered the whole alphabet, Abbie at A and me at Z for Zadie, now we don't, we only go from K to Z. That's ten letters missing. A to E on my left arm, and F to J on my right."

I could hear him thinking.

"I do it with a kitchen knife – I put it under boiling water first, so I'm sure it's safe."

He didn't say anything. I don't remember hearing him fall asleep and I think I must have done before he did.

The next day we went to a phone shop together and bought our first mobile phones. Stuart sent me my first ever text message in the afternoon:

Remember: unlikely things R still possible

I changed my phone two years ago, but I still have that phone, in a shoe box in a cupboard in the flat, because I saved that text message onto the memory and like to be sure I still have it somewhere.

13: Chemicals

I remember it like being inside a bubble at the same time as watching it, separate from it and outside it. I remember running to the edge, Brian being right beside me, and it taking no more than a few fast steps to get there. But the way I remember it now also has that rudimentary special effects feel to it – with me facing a camera quite close up, and I'm not really moving my legs at all apart from jiggling them on the spot, certainly not actually running anywhere, just windmilling my arms about on the spot and making 'oh no!' type expressions with my eyebrows and mouth, and all the while the background is doing swirly patterns on a black background, like I'm in some kind of time travel tunnel. There's no music to it, just odd bits of ambient 'wuuub, wuuuuuub' noises. Then there's me and Brian turning to look at each other and we're both doing 'oh no' type eyebrows and mouths to each other and our hands are starting to wipe meaninglessly at nothing in front of our faces as the camera starts to zoom slowly in on us, as if we're trapped in our time travel predicament, and right then is where the end title music and the credits would start to come up.

In fact, as we pelted to the end, we both slipped, and we both managed to stop ourselves from falling by grabbing onto the trunks of small trees right near the edge. Both my feet went over the side. What I remember about this bit was feeling the bend in the trunk of the tree, like it was turning into rubber in my hand, and also seeing my feet dangling over the edge, thinking, 'they shouldn't be there, they should be on something.'

"Hey!"

I switched my grip from the first trunk to a larger tree a lunge and a reach away and pulled myself up, so I was now lying down on the ground, but my feet weren't in the middle of the sky anymore.

"Hey!"

"You ok?" I said and rolled over to face Brian.

Brian moved his head so I'd follow what he was looking at.

"Hey!" said Stuart again, with a tiny wave. He was lying on a small ledge just a short drop from where we were.

"What's it like down there then?" I said.

"Actually good," he said, "don't seem to be any broken bones or dead mes down here at all."

"At all?" said Brian, pulling himself up into a sitting position, with his knees bent, looking over the edge.

"What's more," said Stuart, "have you seen that?" and he pointed out over the bowl of the quarry we were in.

We were in a large hollowed out bit of world, with jagged white stone edges all around. It was an area about the size of a football pitch, like an abandoned sunken opera house made by a sophisticated under the ground style ancient civilization.

Apart from the ledge where Stuart was busy being not dead on, the whole of the quarry was flooded in water. We didn't know at the time, but this was a disused cement works. My dad explained that's why the water looked the way it did, it's to do with a chemical reaction with the limestone.

It was like we'd stumbled on a lake where the blue was so sharp and bright that this must be the place where the colour blue first came from; this was how it started, the first blue, the original idea of blue, before it got copied and reproduced in dyes and inks. It was turquoise; turquoise so piercing it almost stung as you looked at it, but didn't hurt. You could almost feel it microscopic needle-thin piercing right through your eyes into your head, like light from a welder's torch. You could imagine that if your eyes weren't there to see it the sheer brightness of the blue would just keep going, out into the sky on and on and on. It was so piercing you could imagine that whatever material you put in the way it would pierce right through, steel, concrete, lead, it would go through everything; until it hit someone else's eyes it would just keep going right to the edge of the universe – then it would pierce through that as well and keep on going.

"It's like a colour from the beginning of history," said Stuart. "I bet this is the kind of blue the Greek gods had on Mount Olympus."

"Like seeing one of the colours they'll have in heaven," I said, making my eyes as wide as I could so this exact blue would flood in and I'd never forget it again, because it was as if I'd dreamt of this colour or seen it somewhere before and now I was just remembering clearly. A scatter of bubbles popped on the surface. I imagined Abbie was swimming underwater.

THE AMAZING ADVENTURES OF NO ONE IN PARTICULAR

Episode 4

I realised I was hungry.

I walked into a shop.

I couldn't decide what to buy.

I pretended I was buying for a stranger.

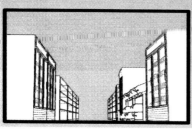

I stood in the checkout queue with my basket.

I remembered I didn't like ham sandwiches.

The girl at the checkout desk was very beautiful.

She just sat and scanned items for ages.

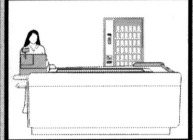

I just stood and watched her.

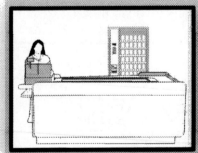

I had a sudden urge to take her with me on the train.

To show her my flat.

And my flatmates.

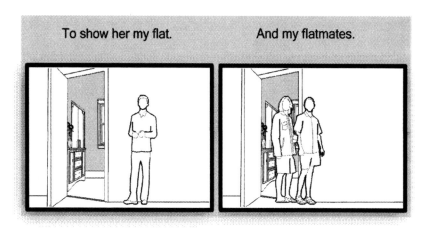

And my other friends.

And the places I liked.

And other places.

A tree I liked.

My local shop.

The stuff I liked doing.

Tell her my secret stuff.

And shower her in all the wonderful stuff
being with me could bring her.

133

And the queue had moved on.

So she scanned my items.

I paid and thanked her.

I left her my ham sandwich.

And she looked at me funny.

To be continued...

Part Five

160 chrctrs

Nyoko Tanaka to Zoe Marowitz

swot happened 2 me 2day: new guy @
work sat @ pc nxt 2 me, 18 20s pipe
cleaner body, ina T-shirt saying 40 wiv a
pic of death on it...

n a silver wedding ring n said he didnt
feel well n only came in coz it was his 1st
day. then i went 4 lunch n came back
took the lift n.

n the fire alarm went n the doors
jammed, there was me n 5 others, n we
pressed the button n nufink so we called
out n tried prising the doors, but...

we cld only open them 3 fingers width n
then they stayed like that. we cld smell
smoke n then...

we cld c smoke n then we couldnt c
NEthing else n then we started coughing
n r eyes started watering n then...

we cld feel the heat from the fire n heard
the glass in the office smashing n all of
us tried to open the doors 2gether...

but they didn't move at all n then we all
started calling as loud as we could n i
started 2 hear my heartbeat in my head
n...

i started 2 think about my mum n how
nice it wld b 2 c her n how she'd only
been dead a month so...

it was a shame not 2 have more new 2
talk about, but really i didn't mind 2
much n i started 2 think about all the
things 2 tell her...

like about how dad hadnt moved her
toothbrush yet n it was still on top of the
sink...

how my nephew looked on his 1st day @
school in his uniform n his new thing 2
say is 'u cheeky devil u!' n...

how my sis has made a book 4 him with
fotos of my mum in n under each 1 it has
things she used 2 say, like...

time 2 climb the wooden mountain, or 2
go 2 bedfudshire, or 2 go by shank's
pony meaning 2 walk or things like that
n...

it just felt like i had all the time i could
ever need 2 think of stuff coz time was
going so slow n...

my mind was going faster, n accelerating
like it was going to break thru a sound
barrier or sum other kind of barrier n...

Sanwar Akram to Animul Hoque

Congratulations! Your number has been
selected as a winner in our Prize Right
draw. To collect your £500 please ring
this number by midnight tonight.

Animul Hoque to Sanwar Akram

That's wot it said, huh? So did u?

Sanwar Akram to Animul Hoque

Wld u?

Animul Hoque to Sanwar Akram

Nah.

Sanwar Akram to Animul Hoque

Nor me. But sum1 at work said they
know sum1 who got a msg like this n
they called, n they answered sum questions
n got the £

Maurice Suckling

Animul Hoque to Sanwar Akram

> I still wldnta rung, even if I knew that
> 1st. Wot sort of questions?

Sanwar Akram to Animul Hoque

> ID, address, phone make, number etc.

Animul Hoque to Sanwar Akram

> Exactly.

Sophie Levin to Glen Holland

> Will never guess whos openg r new renal
> unit 2day?

Glen Holland to Sophie Levin

> I alrdy hrd. She sent press release
> yday.

Sophie Levin to Glen Holland

> O i c. call peoples attn 2 plights of
> 1000s & underfnded hlth srvce?

Glen Holland to Sophie Levin

> Yep. New best of CD out nxt mnth.

Sophie Levin to Glen Holland

> Didnt her dad hve kidny probs?

Glen Holland to Sophie Levin

> Didnt her last CD hover outside top 30?

Freyja King to Connor Robertson

> Hr name was Alice & she went 2 my skool, at 14 we hd a geog class abt rainfrst & she gt upset with tchr & Y wasnt he doing anything 2 help &...

> They hd this argmnt & he snt hr out n b4 she left she sd when she lft skool she was going 2 hlp & hr conscience wld b clear &...

> She did portgse & spnsh lessons after skool. She 1st went out there when she was 18. she went 2 uni & got hr MA in geog. She just won a...

> Schlrshp 2 do conservtn in brazl. She was engagd 2 same byfrnd she hd at skool & they fnd aprtmt there last month &...

> They were back over here 4 hr sis wed nxt wk. I hrd they caught the drvr with infa red cam from a cop helicop - the car was in the grge with door dwn...

The flwrs r still in their wrapper tied 2
the barrier by the bus stop on my way 2
wrk. They been there 4 wks now n r
looking old & u know.

Kiri Bell to Matthew Garrick

U nearly here?

Matthew Garrick to Kiri Bell

No, still here. Im on a bus. Where r u?

Kiri Bell to Matthew Garrick

Im standing by the jetty where the river
cruises go from w8ing 4 u, n sum1 just
asked if I wanted 2 free tickets.

Matthew Garrick to Kiri Bell

Wot u say? Wot they look like?

Kiri Bell to Matthew Garrick

Wool bble hat & matching multi clrd
mits, long blck hair, lil pixie face wiv
tiny red nose, lks like she lives in fashn
mags n is always larfin in wind...

& sun but I said no thanks, coz, well, u
know, but then she asked sum1 else, who

looked like german rockpop star whod
been stretched on a rack & he said...

Ok n him n his m8, who looked the same
but had been squashed got on, & the boat
just left & headed up river.

Matthew Garrick to Kiri Bell

Hmm, well, maybe it's a special sinky
boat n u did the right thing.

Kiri Bell to Matthew Garrick

Maybe but the pixie clths fashn girl got
on it 2.

Matthew Garrick to Kiri Bell

Well i guess so, or otherwise she'd feel
bad about it when it sank.

Nyoko Tanaka to Zoe Marowitz

then we cld hear sum1 outside the lift
calling 4 where we were in the smoke n
we all called out n the voice said 2...

try n prise the doors n we said we'd tried
n the voice said 2 try again n then we saw
the hands come from outside thru the gap
n...

the hands slapped on2 the metal n there
was the ping of metal on metal n i saw
the silver wedding ring n the hands were
spindly n full of tendons n veins n we...

all started 2 pull @ the doors 2 and we
started kickin @ them n the person from
outside started shldr barging n we cld
hear a spring or sumthing n...

there was a clank n 1 of the doors pushed
open n we all sqwezd out like all the time
that had been stored up all came out like
dam burst n all came @ 4x speed...

n new guy went ahead of us n called out
where 2 go 2 get out n asked how many
there were of us n went rnd n made sure
all 5 of us were ok n...

we were coughing n cldnt c n he found
the stairs n the heat was getting less n the
smoke was less thick n then...

we heard him say this way n we heard
the sound of doors smashing open n there
was a rush of colder air n we stumbled
out in2 the carpark n...

as my eyes cleared i cld c all the others
near me on the grnd coffing n splutring n
lying down n other people from the
company rushed up n...

said: wot hppnd 2 u n we said were in lift
n it jammed n they started asking me how
we got out n i said we tried the doors but
no gud but...

the new guy hd come in n helped us n the door gave way n they all went quiet n i looked up n every1 was staring @ me n then sum1 said wot did u say n...

i repeated n every1 looked @ me sum more, carl in accounts with plastic spiky hair n ubertrendy shirts n baby blue puma trainers n...

naomi the producer who they call kebab coz shes so boy popular n they just looked @ me n their mouths guppyfished open n i said wot? n then...

Jack French to Aaron Joyce

I was at my pub but I forgot my wallet so I went back coz its only 2 mins away 2 geddit when this guy outside asked 4 money and

Said he was a builder working on the street and he was from Bristol but his mates had left him by accident taken his coat and he needed 2 get home 2 night and

He looked like a builder but I said, oh really, where in Bristol, coz I'd lived there, and he said redland, and said he just needed

£10 2 get home on the bus coz he had £5 already and then he said he'd be back 2moro 4 work n he'd give me it back then and then

Maurice Suckling

I cld have his bag with his work clothes
in if I wasn't sure about it and I said I
didnt need his bag but he said no, do, he
wld feel better about it, so I did and I
gave him the £10 and

He never turned up the next day, or the
day after or the day after, but 2 weeks
later I was walking near my flat when I
saw him and

Said, hey, remember me, you owe me
£10, i've still got your clothes, u gonna
pay me back? And he said if I met him in
a certain pub at 7

He wld pay me back, but of course I
never went and I chucked his bag in a
skip the next day

Ian Greenough to Martin Stagias

If U R staying in 2night B careful, there
R people walking around and knocking
on doors wanting 2 talk about religion

Martin Stagias to Ian Greenough

CRIPES. YESTDAY IT WAS LABR
PARTY. TURNING LIGHTS & MUSIC
OFF NOW. TA. L8R.

146

Erik Bjorkman to Reku Bjorkman

> I saw someone fall from a building today.
> I heard their head crack on the pavement
> & I saw the dark blood seeping out & I
> went up to them but they weren't
>
> Breathing so i did CPR for 5mins and
> people round me said they were sure he
> was dead and he probably died the
> moment his head hit the pavement and i
> should stop
>
> Because there was nothing i could do but
> I kept trying because i couldn't help it
> and there was a splutter of blood and it
> went all down my white shirt but it
>
> Was only some trapped air and he was
> dead all along and I stopped. When the
> ambulance came it didn't put its sirens on
> when it took him away.

Adam Sanderson to Miles Heath-Patrick

> HOW DID U KNOW HIM?

Miles Heath-Patrick to Adam Sanderson

> MY DAD WAS @ DRAMA SKOL
> WITH HM. DAD SD HE NEVER
> KNEW NE1 WITH MORE NAT
> TALENT, MORE MOTIV8TD &
> MORE LIKLEY 2 SUCCEED

Maurice Suckling

Adam Sanderson to Miles Heath-Patrick

U KID ME?

Miles Heath-Patrick to Adam Sanderson

NO. HE SD HE WAS THE BEST
LOOKING GUY HE'D EVER SEEN,
DID REAL WELL, GOT AGENT
RGHT OUT OF CLGE, WRKED AS
BARMAN DID THTRE BIT PARTS
WALK ONS & MINOR RADIO BITS

Adam Sanderson to Miles Heath-Patrick

THEN WOT?

Miles Heath-Patrick to Adam Sanderson

NOUT. JUST NEVER GOT A BREAK
SO THAT'S WHY HE SELLS
FURNITURE NOW.

Adam Sanderson to Miles Heath-Patrick

I LIKE FURNITURE. U CN SIT ON IT
ETC

Miles Heath-Patrick to Adam Sanderson

SUMHOW I GOT THE IMPRESSION
HE DIDNT LIKE IT MUCH

Adam Sanderson to Miles Heath-Patrick

> U THINK HE TAKES THE
> DISCARDED STOCK AWAY WITH
> HIM IN A VAN AND TAKES IT 2 A
> DESERTED WOOD & HACKS AT IT
> WITH AN AXE TILL ITS ALL IN
> TINY PIECES?

Miles Heath-Patrick to Adam Sanderson

> THEN HE BURIES IT, WEES ON IT,
> AND FEELS ALOT BETTER.

Adam Sanderson to Miles Heath-Patrick

> WHILE SAYING SUMTHING FROM
> A PLAY OR WHATEVER

Miles Heath-Patrick to Adam Sanderson

> NATCH

Adam Sanderson to Miles Heath-Patrick

> NATCH

Tamu Hall to Popo Hall

> U c the paper? Looks like u'r photo?

Maurice Suckling

Popo Hall to Tamu Hall

Is my photo, but they changed it.

Tamu Hall to Popo Hall

Huh? How?

Popo Hall to Tamu Hall

If u look careful u can c shadow on face doesn't match the shadow on body.

Tamu Hall to Popo Hall

She wasnt with those people then?

Popo Hall to Tamu Hall

The photo it came from was when she was in a supermarket carpark 3 yrs earlier.

Janet Grey to Guy Milton

U rember person yday wiv the hair scraped back so far u cld c her scalp + asked 4 50p 2 get a train?

Guy Milton to Janet Grey

Yep, who told long story about her bag + fone being stolen?

150

Janet Grey to Guy Milton

> Yep. Just seen her again + she told me
> exact same thing again

Guy Milton to Janet Grey

> What u say 2 her?

Janet Grey to Guy Milton

> U said that 2 me yday - she said i still
> aint been home yet

Guy Milton to Janet Grey

> Yeah right

Janet Grey to Guy Milton

> Sho was still in same clothes mind

Nyoko Tanaka to Zoe Marowitz

> Kerry said, nyoko, that never hpnd, then
> erik from IT came n asked me questions
> coz he does 1st aid, n i told him wot
> hpnd, n he said...
>
> that new guy hd been taken away by
> amblance, he got trapped by fire on top
> floor n tried getting out on the roof, but
> 100odd people saw him fall n he
> landed...

on the pavement, n his head made a loud
noise n he showed me where n it was
dark red wiv blood n the other 5 from the
lift didn't...

say a word - we all just looked. r now in
a pub rnd crner on r own. no1 is spking,
just drinking. i am ok but havent spoken
yet. x

Zoe Marowitz to Nyoko Tanaka

On way 2 find u. xxx

Chicken Supreme Ready Meal

"The...face...of...Jesus...is...on...my.........chicken breasts." I said it real slow, my knife and fork in my hands hovering in mid air, my eyes locked on and not moving.

"He's on my chicken breasts – AJ, you gotta see this." I dunno why but I stood up then, as if a controly part of my body knew it was an occasion when sitting was wrong. As a result, this set Alien off.

"Alien! Quiet! No! No!" I snapped.

We'd had Alien for four months by this point and weren't making a whole lotta progress. When anyone stood up, or when anyone touched anyone else, or when anyone opened any kind of door, even a kitchen cabinet door, but not the washing machine door, she went chicken oriental-mental. She was scared of the washing machine. First time she saw it go on you could see her head going round trying to follow it. Shortly after the fast spin part of the wash cycle I came into the kitchen to find her in a ball, with a puddle of sick by her, making tiny whimpering noises. Ever since, when the washing machine has gone on, she's left the room.

There must have been the same kind of controly bit in AJ too, coz he stood up as well, and he hadn't even seen it yet. Course, this set Alien off more.

"Alien, no! Down! Get down!" I shouted, though she always took less notice of me – she preferred boys.

"Alien! Basket!" shouted AJ, and her tail wagging slowed down, even if her face still looked manic. She stood for a bit longer and when AJ pointed she did a couple of turns on the spot, hung her eyelids at us, showed us her sad face, then went to her basket, circled once then flopped into it like a comma.

"See, it is, isn't it!" I turned the plate to AJ, who took a kind of step back, then took one forward and stared at it.

There it was plainly, the bearded face in the glaze of the creamy sauce over the pieces of chicken, the intense yet kind eyes rendered by two pieces of mushroom, the nostrils by near adjacent pieces of ham. Because the dish comes served on a bed of long grain patna rice it doesn't sit flat, so the image could only be seen from a certain angle, with light falling a certain way. AJ had to move the dish into the light a little, then duck his head down, so it was pretty much the height my head had been as I sat about to eat it. He nudged the plate into position twice, then locked onto it. I scanned his face for clues as he focussed on the chicken.

"Kish...," he said, all slow and thoughtful, (Kish, like the sound you make to mean glass breaking, because of clumsiness, though everyone else calls me Sarah, or school friends call me Sarah G-String), "...it's...not... Jesus...it's...a Bee Gee."

"It's Jesus, AJ, and it's a sign!"

"It's not, it's a Bee Gee." He was ramping up the volume now. This kicked Alien off again.

"It's not a Bee Gee, what kind of sign would that be?" I was starting to yell.

"Don't be so down on the Bee Gees the whole time." Now he was angry and he took it out on Alien.

"Alien! Be quiet!"

"I'm not, I respect them a great deal, they were untouchable at their zenith." I could feel my fists clenching.

"You don't mean that, so why say it?" We had now reached Neighbours Can Hear levels, and Alien had started jumping up and doing broken laps of us.

"I fucking well do mean it. Legend has it they wrote *Tragedy*, *Too Much Heaven* and *How Deep Is Your Love* all in one afternoon! How could I possibly not respect that!?!?" I jutted my face towards his.

"Then maybe you can explain to me why they didn't feature in the mix CD you did for Holly last week – not one Bee Gee track on a whole disco compilation. How is that possible?" The palms of AJ's hands opened out wide, and he hadn't finished:

"More than any other band they almost are Disco! I mean, yes," and here he started to list the names on his fingers, "you found a place, rightly so, for Lipsync and *Funkytown*, yes Shannon and *Let the Music Play*, yes Abba and *Dancing Queen*, Donna Summer, Earth Wind and Fire, Chic, Patti Labelle, Chaka Khan, Boney M, James Brown, yes, yes, yes, yes, yes, yes, yes but..." he held his hands out to stop me trying to butt in, "...you and I both know this goes back to the argument we had at your mum's house, no let me finish, to the argument we had at your mum's house last year when you you, incredulously – I still can't believe you said it – you said, and everyone heard you say it, you preferred the *Boogie Box High* – aka George Michael – aka Andros Georgious – cover version of 1987, over the 1975 classic – and it seems clear to me that this is a continuation of that argument, perpetuated by the censorship – yes censorship – that you are inflicting on Holly's restricted knowledge base of the genre."

He folded his arms.

"Alien! Down!" yelled AJ again, turning away from me.

I hand on hipped him, and, in the pop of the moment I think I also turkey-necked him sista style and matched him for volume, because I had to, or I would have lost:

"That compilation was in no way designed to be an overview, complete or otherwise of the genre, no, now let me finish, you didn't like it when I did it to you, in no way designed to be an overview, complete or otherwise of the genre, it was intended purely as a personal reflection of current favourites and all time favourites, not you will have noted if you had looked more closely at the track-listing of *Holly's* CD..."

"It was on when we went round..."

"I haven't finished!"

"It was your handwriting!"

"I haven't finished!" I upped my volume again.

"If you had looked more closely at the track listing of *Holly's* CD, you would have noted that Salt 'n' Peppa's massive 1986 *Push It*, Madonna's 1985 *Into the Groove*, Deee-lite's 1990 *Groove is in the Heart* and Dusty Springfield's peerless 1968 Memphis session recording of *Breakfast in Bed* – hardly, I think you will agree, hardly constituting a Disco compilation at large!"

And then I know I turkey-necked him.

Maurice Suckling

He said nothing.

"Anyway," I hollered, waving my hands in front of my face, "it's not a fucking Bee Gee, look at it, fucking look at it – it's the face of Jesus and it's a sign!"

"Bee Gee!" he shouted, making his teeth clench right after.

"You're not looking!" I went to pick the plate up, bring it right up under his nose, get him to really really look, but it sorta slipped out of my fingers before I'd got a proper hold of it and it spun round and smashed onto the kitchen floor. Within a second Alien was onto it, scoffing down my dinner as we stood by speechless.

That night AJ had his chicken. It didn't have any kind of picture on it. I heated up a pizza from the freezer. A few days later a friend of mine from work suggested looking in Alien's poo to see if the sign was still there. I don't think she was being serious, but I think I would've looked if it had occurred to me sooner.

We had had this dish lots before. It is the Birds Eye 375g frozen ready meal. 13% of it is chicken. 50% is rice and the rest is other stuff – water mostly.

For Christmas last year our present from my old school friend Fluffy was an 850 watt microwave. In this, the bag of rice only takes 4 minutes. It needs to be left to stand for 2 minutes, which is perfect because the chicken and sauce bag takes 2 minutes, so if you do the rice first, the timings work out perfect.

I went back to the same store and bought all eighteen of the dishes in stock in the freezer cabinet. We had one each a day for the next nine days on the trot, but the same thing never happened again. I bought another eighteen. We got through two of them each, without any results, then AJ started throwing up whenever he smelt it, so we decided to stop there which was probably the right decision because food had got very dull and evening meals had developed into a no one speaks to each other ordeal. Alien ate all the next eleven, left most of the twelfth, then never touched the thirteenth, and we threw the last one out.

Almost three months to the day after that one went in the bin – and you always wonder if that was going to be the one – we both had an Italian Chicken and Asparagus Carbonara when AJ's Orrechietti pasta formed on the plate into shapes that looked a bit like the profile of a sister of a friend of ours who works for Habitat. We took photos of it

156

with my new digital camera and we showed people and emailed it to everyone we could think of, but no one else thought it looked like anyone at all.

Disposable Planet

-------Original Message-------
From: Catalina Fernandez
Sent: 24 August 2006 11:07
To: Russ Sillar
Subject: not saying

I am so bored.
There's nothing to do here today. They're supposed to be having meetings to decide what to do with our department. That was supposed to happen two weeks ago.
I am so bored.
When's bird flu supposed to come kill us?
What you doing?

-------Original Message-------
From: Russ Sillar
Sent: 24 August 2006 11:19
To: Catalina Fernandez
Subject: RE: not saying

I am so busy.
Did I ever send you this? From 19th August 2002.
12 reasons to move planet.
If you've got time you could start looking for a place to go.

http://news.bbc.co.uk/hi/english/static/in_depth/world/2002/disposable_planet/slideshow/img12.stm

Maurice Suckling

Links 1 to 12 read:

Population
In the next 10 years about 800 million people will be added to the global population.

Food
Food production will have to nearly double to meet the demands of this growth.

Cities
At the beginning of the last century, only one in 10 people lived in cities. Now it's close to 50% – and it's still rising.

Pollution
Half the world's urban residents are exposed to potentially harmful amounts of sulphur dioxide, ozone and particulate matter in "smogs".

Biodiversity
Every year thousands of species become extinct due to human activity and the loss of natural habitat.

Forestry
Logging and land conversion to accommodate human demand has shrunk the world's forests by half.

Wetlands
Urban and industrial development claimed half the world's wetlands in the 20th Century.

Water
Within 25 years, half the world's population could have trouble finding enough fresh water for drinking and irrigation.

Refugees

By 2025, the number of refugees fleeing floods and natural disasters could quadruple to 100 million.

Energy

For global development to be both fair and sustainable, the rich world may need to cut energy and resource use by 90% by 2050.

Transport

In the last 20 years there has been a two-thirds increase in global household energy use, road vehicle fleets have doubled, and air traffic has quadrupled.

Waste

As population, consumption and wealth increase, so does the quantity of waste we produce. The rich countries of the OECD produce an annual total of almost two tonnes of waste for every person.

-------Original Message------
From: Catalina Fernandez
Sent: 24 August 2006 11:36
To: Russ Sillar
Subject: disposable planet

11 reasons to move. I like cities.
I found this:

http://news.bbc.co.uk/1/hi/world/americas/3002680.stm

Link reads:
Space trips up for grabs
The US company which helped put the first two tourists in space says it is ready to start selling tickets for its first solely commercial trip in 2005.

Maurice Suckling

The company – Space Adventures – will be charging $20m a person for the roughly 10-day trip to the International Space Station.

-------Original Message-------
From: Russ Sillar
Sent: 24 August 2006 12:04
To: Catalina Fernandez
Subject: RE: disposable planet

Maybe we should go see a comedy tonight for cheering up?

-------Original Message-------
From: Catalina Fernandez
Sent: 24 August 2006 12:06
To: Russ Sillar
Subject: RE: disposable planet

Or work on a business plan to raise the $40m?

-------Original Message-------
From: Russ Sillar
Sent: 24 August 2006 12:44
To: Catalina Fernandez
Subject: RE: disposable planet

Cry?

-------Original Message-------
From: Catalina Fernandez
Sent: 24 August 2006 12:45
To: Russ Sillar
Subject: RE: disposable planet

Sex?

-------Original Message-------
From: Russ Sillar
Sent: 24 August 2006 12:46
To: Catalina Fernandez
Subject: RE: disposable planet

You win.

-------Original Message-------
From: Catalina Fernandez
Sent: 24 August 2006 12:47
To: Russ Sillar
Subject: RE: disposable planet

Try and get home on time.
I'll be wearing nothing.
Except a brand new (recycled) pair of green wellies.

Story Translated From Bleeps From Outer Space

"Galaxy of tripe!" exclaimed Zargo, "I thought we'd bought it that time." His long green tentacles clung to the controls of his white one-seater space-ship as it came out of an emergency roll. Other tentacles mopped his brow, whilst others fixed his goggles to his head, and others set the framed photo of his wife and child upright again in the cockpit.

"Borx, old man, are you clipped?" One of his eyes looked around him at the control panel, reading the dials and meters and readouts. Another eye looked behind him to get a sighting of the red ship that had fired on him without warning, whilst another one looked into the empty space ahead, as he worked out an escape plan.

"Oh, don't you worry about me, old man," said the steady digitised voice of the ship's computer. "It's just a flesh wound." Then the computer shut down and smoke gushed from the mainframe on the dashboard. Dead.

"****!"[1] yelled Zargo as he smashed a clenched tentacle into the control panel. A flash of anger in his three eyes, and the three antennae on the top of his head straightened like three rigid aerials. Then they relaxed, drooped a little and bobbed slightly, as a colder, more dangerous look of anger filled his eyes.

A light on the control panel showed the radio still worked. He had a call. He already knew who it was.

"Are you ready to die?" snarled the cruel dry voice.

Vark, his nemesis.

---

[1] Literally: 'piece of excrement from a Bluurgephant.'

Maurice Suckling

For 14,000 years Zargo and Vark had duelled each other through the skies and interplanetary space of Porthaldown 9 and the Spurran Sector of the Tartan Galaxy. Zargo was trying to find his way back home to Formica 6. It had seemed to Zargo and Borx as if the whole universe was trying to stop them from getting home. They had been attacked by space pirates, sung to by space whelks with mesmerising voices and been trapped on that planet for centuries. After that, they had just taken off from a planet mere minutes before it was swallowed whole by a space whale. Zargo had been unintentionally poisoned by the special on the space brunch menu. They had narrowly escaped a crash with a floating pilot-less hopelessly ancient hulk of a ship with pictures of a mostly hair-less species on the side, seemingly a male and a female, with an address appearing to indicate a tiny blue planet in the Milky Way on it. The species reminded Zargo of food he'd eaten in a restaurant once, where he had too much white wine, was very ill and never returned.

Vark, like Zargo, was also returning from the Microwave Wars. The two had been on opposite sides in the war, and Zargo had killed Vark's brother in a dogfight in skies over a sock factory. But unlike Zargo, Vark had no family to return to, and was filled with bitterness and hatred of Zargo. Vark had made it his life to hunt down and kill his enemy, no matter where he went.

"You will never get back to Formica 6 without a computer," said Vark's cruel voice over the intercom.

Zargo knew it.

"Now listen here, you fiend," said Zargo, "I'm not the sort of fellow to throw in the towel when he receives a bloody nose."

"Admit it, Zargo. You're race is run. Only the Dungaree People can save you now."

Zargo knew it.

"You're a cad, sir. A bounder. In fact, hang it, sir. You're a ****."[2]

As he said the word Zargo already knew one of Vark's tentacles would lunge for the button to fire the laser to finish him off.

---

[2] Literally: 'an area related to the female reproductive system of a Nurdledile.'

With the scorching red laser shooting through the distance between the two ships, Zargo sent his ship into a steep dive and flicked to Random Hyper Space. The red laser burst in the space where Zargo's ship had just left only a fraction of a second before. In the intense pressure of the jump to random hyper space Zargo lost consciousness. He dreamt of a black sea of tiny stars. He was looking for something, but the sea was too big, too dark. He was looking for one star among the many, but all the stars were too tiny and he couldn't tell them apart. He woke lost and exhausted, with a new kind of emptiness. He missed the voice of his computer, Borx.

Zargo drifted through space for several decades. Space is almost entirely nothing, and it doesn't half go on about it. He drifted through meteor fields and planets that were so bright and aluminous green they reminded him of home. He landed on a few, but the similarity to Formica 6 made it hard for him to stay long. He replenished his supplies, made makeshift repairs to his spaceship, then left. Without Borx, his ship limped from place to place, unable to perform standard operations. The hyper space jump had rendered it further debilitated. Without Borx, many essential functions simply didn't work, or Zargo was forced to construct temporary solutions that had no hope of making it past the outer ring of the current galaxy, wherever that may be. He had used his last cereal packet box to construct makeshift landing gear and he had used his in-flight CDs to make a solar panel to help power his failing ship. But there was nothing he could do about the dwindling supply of carbon dioxide into the cockpit.

He was half delirious with lack of food, when he saw the blue denim planet. He knew at once what it was, but didn't trust any of his eyes. He knew what he wanted it to be, second only to one other planet, but didn't know if he could allow himself to believe it. When it's through with indifference, space can be cruel, and Zargo knew it. He approached the planet cautiously. The atmosphere was dense with a white misty smoke. He put the landing gear into action. The wheels buckled under the weight of the ship. If this wasn't the planet Zargo needed it to be, this would be the last planet he would ever land on. In the skid along the dusty surface, Zargo lost consciousness before he hit the rivet polishing building complex.

Zargo woke to see several beautiful females wearing nothing

Maurice Suckling

except dungarees, engine grease over their sweaty brown forearms, and across their foreheads. He was in a bed. The smell of fresh sweat pumped through the air, awakening senses that had been asleep for so long Zargo had forgotten them. Each cell nudged the others next to it to wake up and pay attention.

"I say, what-ho, am I dead?" he said.

"Another week in that wreck and you would have been," said the most beautiful and sweatiest and most covered in engine grease of all the females there. Zargo smiled three smiles, one on top of the other. He knew he was going to be ok.

In mere weeks, he was ready to leave. The Dungaree People had repaired his ship beyond a state of newness. Zargo had witnessed their legendary powers in mechanics at first tentacle. He had been there when they first fired the replacement jet boosters. He had been there when they first tested the upgrade to the front firing lasers. He had been there when Borx first spoke again.

It took him two days to shake tentacles with every one of the Dungaree People as he set out to say goodbye. All of them were females, all semi-un-dressed the same, and as he went through the town, taking turns to rest his other tentacles, he thought how each female was even more beautiful, and sweaty and more covered in engine grease than the next. He thought about his wife and the tiny planet where he hoped she was still waiting for him. As he came to the last of his goodbyes, with the female who had spoken to him on the day he woke in the hospital bed. He stood for a moment, as the topic that had been puzzling him for some time refused to go away.

"Look here, old chap...one...hesitates to mention such a thing...but...by all appearances...you and your men...all appear to be...well, frankly...females," he said politely, hesitantly.

"Yes, Zargo, we are." She wiped the back of her hand across her forehead, leaving a sweaty black mark there to glisten in the daylight.

"Ah, I see, righto..., then..." Zargo didn't know how to frame the question.

"We reproduce by *******"[3], she said.

---

[3] No direct translation available. The word appears to mean a technique involving some kind of improvised culinary implement.

168

Dazed, Zargo held out a tentacle to shake. The mechanic leant forward and kissed him, the strap of her dungarees slipping down over her rounded brown shoulder as she did so. Slightly shaken Zargo got in his ship and stood at the open cockpit.

"Tally ho," he waved, sat down, shut the cockpit, and took off. For the next 3,000 years certain images took up residence in all his brains. He felt unfaithful to his wife. He frequently thought of turning round, going back to the planet, and asking if he could watch.

One day, if it was day, because in space everything is permanently 3am in the morning, a small yellow planet honed into view.

"According to my software, old chap," said Borx, "that there is Yellow Rock – gateway to the Yellow Galaxy."

"I say," said Zargo. "Jolly well done, and those two yellow planets there just behind…by all accounts they ought to be…"

"Nylon 1 and Nylon 2, old chap," said Borx, with a happy note in his digital voice, "all we have to do now is follow them."

Zargo thought of his wife. He thought of his baby, who had barely had a tentacle when he had left for the wars. By now that child may have children of its own, all green and slimy.

Borx thought of a dishwasher he had rejected before leaving for the wars. Where once it had seemed to him so unadventurous and inhibited, now its simple domesticity and good intentions seemed so welcome and he dared to hope it was still operational yet unattached.

When seconds later the red space ship cruised into view in front of them, with the calmness of a long prepared menace, neither spoke at first. It seemed inevitable Vark would be there.

In the time it took to close the distance between the two ships, Borx had readied all the armaments and engaged the defence shield. The whole ship was at maximum battle-readiness. A steady calm expression fell across Zargo's forehead as he lowered his goggles for battle.

The two ships were now so close to each other, directly facing, hovering in space, that Zargo could see his opponent. A thin slimy green creature in a black uniform. The visor on his black helmet was still raised.

Zargo pressed a button on the control panel and spoke.

"Vark, I call upon you to step aside sir. No more slime need be shed. We two have done honour enough to the microchips of war. Step aside, sir, and let us duel no more."

Silence in space goes on forever.

Vark lowered his visor.

"Vark," said Zargo again, "you have been my esteemed enemy all these long years, but now let us put the wars behind us. You have done honour in the wars, and done honour to your brother…"

As Vark fired, Zargo had already put his ship into a dive, so that within seconds he was underneath Vark's ship and starting to loop back round as it climbed. Vark had hardly moved, too shocked by the speed and skill of Zargo and his ship, too sure that he had rendered the ship un-manoeuvrable on their last encounter. Now behind Vark's ship, flying upside down, Zargo released two pulses from his front firing lasers. Two hits and Vark's ship was on fire and spiralling into a death dive.

Zargo watched it as it plummeted.

Radio static.

"Zargo!" Vark was in difficulties, it sounded as if the ship was moments from breaking up.

"Zargo! You must have found the Dungaree People," yelled Vark, "did no one ever tell you about the virus? Wohhaaaaaaaaaaa."

Explosion.

Debris swirled out from where the ship had been, each piece looping over itself as it spun away from the centre of the blast, slowing up, looping in slower and slower circles, as space reverted to the calm of its perpetual nothingness once again.

On the journey back to Formica 6 Borx launched a search of his database.

> *Physical contact with the Dungaree*
> *People transmits an incurable virus.*
> *Travelers with this virus are*
> *permanently barred from entry on all*
> *planets in the Yellow, Green and Blue*
> *galaxies.*

For the rest of their natural lives Zargo and Borx orbit the planet Formica 6. Zargo can see its distinctive bright aluminous green seas that cover most of its surface. He can see the shape of its blue lands and make out the larger of its biggest red cities. He can't see the town where his family are because it's too small, but he thinks he knows where it is. When he orbits the planet when he's asleep, just as he passes directly over the place where his family are, the three antennae on the top of his head stand up as straight as ever they can, then, a second later, as the path of the orbit takes him away, the antennae droop down again.

His slimy green wife, as ever, continues to look up at the stars at night and makes wishes on them. Even when she is drying up and her green is fading, she continues to do the same. On one particular occasion, the star that she wishes on is in fact his spaceship, orbiting right above her.

THE AMAZING ADVENTURES OF NO ONE IN PARTICULAR

Episode 5

So I took my lunch and walked.

And walked.

And I tried to find a place to eat it.

Nowhere seemed right, so I kept on walking.

Then I noticed a hill.

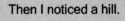

So I decided to walk there.

I could picture myself sat at the top of it...

...eating my lunch, looking down at this random city...

...and feeling OK about it.

And the thought of feeling OK about it...

...made me feel more OK about it.

Then I nearly trod in some dog shit.

It was just on the pavement.

Like an exclamation mark in a curly brown font...

...sat right in my way.

But I didn't tread in it.

There was a time I was with James.

And he saw some dog shit.

And I didn't.

But he warned me.

And I jumped out of the way.

176

Part Six

Infinite Things To Do With Microwaves

1. CDs

Prop up with something glass or plastic (not metal) so they stand up and face screen. Patterns. Like an alien's brainwaves. (Don't inhale gas.)

Bike With Dog Attached

He was like his dog. His dog was wiry and jumpy, mid-sized, a jet-black coat, a thick silver chain round the neck, and unpredictable. Just like him. When his dog made a lunge for a boy on a bike in the very same park a few months earlier he managed to drag it away by the lead. The tyre was punctured by the dog's teeth, and the boy was spooked. So now you could tell the difference between them easier, because the dog was the one with the muzzle, and he was the other one.

And yet now, walking in the park in a late summer evening, the light holding out like it might not bother to go at all and just stay till morning, the smell of new mown grass in the air, seemingly no one else around, he takes the muzzle off.

And now, minutes later, this is when the dog sees something that sparks its anger, and this time shakes loose the grip on its lead, and it can't be stopped, getting closer, closer as it hacks out demented barks. And there are its teeth. Teeth. Teeth.

2. Soap

It lathers and distorts. And grows. And grows.

ExperiMental

Today I saw one, and it was of the most top variety – the dementedly content face, the long flapping tongue – excellent. It was over almost as soon as it began because the car was going quite a bit faster than ours on the outside lane. I was driving so I saw more of it than Finn who was in the seat next to me. We recorded it in our Book of Sightings still, and dated it and placed it as accurately as we could, because even if you only get a second, as long as you see their face you know it counts. On the map of the UK in our spare room we placed the redheaded pin to mark the place.

There was a time, when we were ExperiMental, and we both knew we were. I think even then we both knew it couldn't keep going on the way it was: something was going to happen, either we stopped on our own, or we'd get blown up and be stopped by something else.

3. Toothpicks
Stand up and light end (can use a cork). Fireballs shoot out end and watch for bursts of changing colour.

Buy The Cheapest Ones You Can Find (With High Wattage)
Finn and I both worked in the same graphic design studio, which was how we met, so we used to leave together. When we moved in together we went to work and left together as well. We used to go to work, drink too much on weeknights sometimes, drink too much at weekends always, watch too much TV, look for other jobs, talk of moving somewhere else but never take the first step to even begin, and we used to put things in microwaves that you weren't supposed to. Lots of things. We'd do this sober. We'd do this drunk. We'd do it in the morning before leaving for work. We'd email each other during the day with ideas for things to try and predictions for what we thought might happen. We'd get home, put things in, watch them, film them with a digital camera, and save them onto our computer at home, date them, and add comments. We took days off work to get things on purpose, just to try them out. Gel ice packs for cooler boxes – explosion. A Polaroid camera: use the photo not the camera. There are a very large number of things in the world. Very many of them fit inside a microwave. It's good to have a hobby; but bad when it has you.

When we did an egg and our first microwave blew up and the door flew off we just went out and got another one. We lost our second when we got ball lightning off a large candle, and that blew the door off too.

But there was never any question of us stopping just because of a couple of doors blowing off. We both knew that somewhere out there was something that would have to stop us, but it was nothing we could imagine, or even wanted to try to, because microwaving was our thing. Microwaving was us.

4. Polaroid Photo
Soon as you take it put it in for 2 secs. Sparks. Take it out. Startling colours.

Bury Your Microwaves For The Future
So it came to be that the work to which we were called required of us to bury our beloved microwave in the grounds of the local park at night, while it smelt of freshly mown summer grass. Our microwave was to be a time capsule, a means to pass on the message we had been entrusted with.

Inside our last ever microwave, as per our instructions, was a watertight, airtight Tupperware box and inside that was the sheet of paper on which we had recorded our list of advice to the people of the future. The future is the most important thing, because it is has a purpose. The future is where heaven is getting built.

5. Grapes
Cut one in half, but leave a tiny slither of skin between them. Place both halves face down. Arcs of light from one half to the other. (Some unreliability, but persevere for results.)

Black Dog White Teeth
We realised we should have perhaps left it till later as soon as we got to the park. But we reasoned that it would soon get darker, and anyway, there was no one around because it was later than it looked.

By a cluster of trees at the edge of the park, we dug a hole in the hard summer earth that went down the length of our spade. We patted the earth back down, wondering how likely it was people would spot it, arguing for and against each other as we debated the point.

And so it came to be that we were walking back to the car, our tools over our shoulders, when the dog came at us. Tearing up the ground under its feet, scampering at us faster than we could think, the black dog, blacker even than the background it was hurtling out of, silhouetted against the sky, pulled up just short of us to let out a battery of barks. And that is when we saw the awfulness of its white white teeth.

It dipped its head and snarled, then lunged straight for Finn's throat.

6. Light bulbs

They glow, as if they were on, but brighter, and more colours. Then they blow out. Strange frosting effect. They grow bits out of them like tumours.

That Day

We woke up a minute before our alarm went off and felt refreshed. All our clothes were just where we'd hoped to find them. Our favourites all clean and freshly aired.

We opened a fresh new carton of orange juice, which we'd already put in the fridge. We opened a new fresh carton of cooled milk for our cereal. Finn got a tax rebate. I got a much belated birthday present from my sister we were all convinced had got lost in the post.

"Shall we?" said Finn, pointing with his eyes over to the microwave.

"Save it?"

"That's what I was thinking," he said.

We drove to work, starting with an almost full tank of petrol. The engine fired first time. All sixteen of the sets of lights between work and home were green. Every song on the radio was one of our favourites. We got our favourite parking space at work. The talk that day was of everybody's bonuses. We did far better than either of us could have expected. At lunchtime we went to our favourite café, and the waitress we thought had left served us, and gave us a free side salad.

My computer didn't crash once that day. I wasn't stuck in a printer queue, I never once had to reload the printer with paper or ink. Twice I went into the kitchen to find the kettle had just boiled and there was enough hot water for me. On both those occasions I also found a clean teaspoon, and enough sugar in the bowl and none of it was wet and brown and clumped together. I got an email from a friend whose email address I'd lost and not heard from for nearly two years.

On the drive back home all sixteen traffic lights were green again, and there was hardly any traffic at all on our roads.

When we got back to the flat the ugly armchair that had been outside in the rain for the last six weeks, which a neighbour had dumped, had finally been taken away somewhere.

As we walked into the kitchen we stopped, took in the sight and looked at each other.

"You know this is a miracle, don't you," said Finn

We both took small steps towards it. I stooped down, crouching, balancing on my toes. I started moving a hand over the debris, picking at pieces of it, putting them into my other hand.

"Come on, Fox! You know this is! You know it! This is what the whole day was building towards! This! This is it!"

"So what does it mean, then Tiger?" I said, looking up at him.

Finn crouched down next to me, and put his hand over the top of my picking up hand.

"It means, Fox, it means it's time to stop."

I looked from his hand on my hand, to his face.

"Yes, yes, it is, isn't it."

There seemed no reason why the microwave should have fallen off the worktop during the day and smashed on the kitchen floor. We were sure we'd left it tucked back against the wall when we'd tried an old printer ink cartridge in it the night before. Maybe we hadn't put it back right. Maybe it had got knocked in the morning.

"So what do we do with it?" I said.

"We wait for that to be clear," said Finn scrunching up his brow.

"And what do we do instead…you know, instead of…"

"Takeaway?" suggested Finn.

7. Pins with coloured plastic heads
Sparks out the ends. Heads melt. (Use glass plate in future.)

We Are Called
That night Finn bolted up in bed, dead on 4am.

"What is it, Tiger?…You ok?"

"I just had a dream, Fox, only it was one of those that felt so real I was sure it was happening."

"Your back is covered in sweat."

"We were watching the fire shoot off a scouring pad in the

Maurice Suckling

microwave, when we saw a face in the flames. I couldn't place it but I knew I knew it.

"It said:

Go place your microwave under the soil of the earth. Surf not on these radiation waves for evermore.

And within your microwave you are to place a written page – A4 is fine, and it's ok to fold it – of sincere advice to the people of the future who will find your time capsule and fall down in wonder and in worship.

Go now, and be not sarcastic. Go now, and be wise and know that you have spoken with...

"That's when the scourer burned up and the flame went out."

8. Crisp Packet

Turned inside out. Green, blue, silver flares. They can catch light too.

The Dog That Didn't

The dog lunged at Finn, and in the half dark it was hard to see how it happened. But it went very quiet, as if the sound had stopped completely. Then I remember the faintest sound of paw pads landing back on the grass, and the sound came back in. Finn patted the dog on the head and told it that it was good. It whimpered, then chased round in a circle quite slowly several times.

We left it standing there in the park, wagging its black tail silhouetted against the dark dark blue almost black sky. It barked out a single goodbye.

9. Marshmallows

They grow.

New Collection

So now, instead of microwaving, we spend our spare time logging our sightings, taking photos if we can and storing all the data on our computer and marking the locations on the master map in the spare bedroom.

There's nowhere really you can go to be sure to get a sighting, though we do drive to dog shows most months. We don't ever get out, we just drive there before the start, do something nearby if we feel like hanging around, then drive back with the rest of the traffic.

10. Frozen Chillies

They spark and flame and set alight.

Advice to People of the Future

Dear People of the Future, do you still speak English? We're guessing it's some kind of Chinese derived language, but we're sure you're very smart and will be able to translate this ok.

The year is 2004. If you discover time travel you can find us at the address on the back of the attached photo most weekends. Please come visit anytime. If you do discover it, please feel free to use the machine you have just found to do experiments with using an infinite variety of things you find across the universe. We have enclosed our logbooks for your interest. Also, still on the subject, be very careful about de-frosting the cryogenically frozen people from our time – they are not truly representative of our society, which largely considers them to be egocentrically unbalanced freaks with more money than good ideas for songs to play at a funeral.

We have put our two heads together (again see attached photo of us – these aren't the real colours we had in our world at the time – we made the colours with the machine) and come up with the following list of life advice. We hope it may be useful to you.

If you have become extinct (our guesses, in no order, are: nuclear, terrorism, climate change, computers take over, lack of grammar, over-fixation with grammar, mobile phones turn out to be bad) then please ignore this note.

1.   Clean underwear everyday, isn't just healthy, but makes you feel generally better about yourself too.
2.   No one likes a show off.
3.   No one likes a grumbler.
4.   Don't mix beer and wine.
5.   Grow your own herbs at home, it's easy and fun and makes you feel smart.
6.   If you've just moved into a new place carry a tape measure around with you the whole time.
7.   Always have a book (if you still have them) with you when you travel – helps make you feel like no time is wasted if you're delayed.

Maurice Suckling

8.   Never attempt sarcasm in emails (if you still have them).
9.   Have a glass of water by your bed every night, in case you
        wake up thirsty.
10.   Get a car (if you still have them) and put a dog (if you still
         have them) inside, wind down the window for it, drive at
        speed, and this is VERY IMPORTANT, watch the expression
        on its face. Life on earth honestly doesn't get much better
        than this. If you do come and visit we'll show you our
        logbook and photos.

Hope everything is ace.
Best wishes
Finlay R Langley & Laura H Fredericks
(From the past.)

Two Incidents Several Years Apart

I am walking by the cloudy brown river late afternoon, with my plastic supermarket carrier bags stretching with bought things.

I see the most amazing white swan.

How *white* this swan is. It's a shocking white. The white the whole world was before the rest of it was coloured in. It's good to be on the same planet as something so white. I feel an amazingness as sparkling as angels tip-toeing over the surface of the earth. If it starts to fly right in front of me my heart will burst and a tramp will get lucky when he finds my carrier bags with shopping in.

I get nearer. I see it isn't a swan. It's a piece of industrial waste.

All my amazingness goes away.

Amazingness is better than reality.

*

Years pass. I change jobs. Move house. Get promotion. Buy more technology. Buy a car with air conditioning. Feel stuck. Break up with Emma. Take up hill walking. Miss Emma so much almost every night I dream I'm dead and the dreams feel good and become my things to look forward to.

*

I find the stream through a clearing. It's quiet, but that isn't it. It's the water that does it. That water is so clear. All I can do is look at it.

I can see the pebbles at the bottom. I can see the thin green water plants sway in slow motion. I can even see a fish with the spots on its grey skin.

The water is just so clear it does me in.

I know I should go soon. Find the car. Drive back. Open the front door. Sleep. Get up. Do the things I do.

If anyone saw me I would look just the same to them. From the outside no one could know how everything had changed, unless they too had once seen water this clear.

The Spark of Divinely Random Intervention

Strike 1

There were rumours about what happened to you if you were caught escaping. Dovetail, real name Bruce, who always had a strong smell of chemicals about him, said you were thrown in battery acid and your body dissolved without a trace. Flightstar, real name Hailey (always slept with the light on and talked about the dimensions of fitted kitchens in her sleep) said you were taken deep into the forest and shot or stabbed and buried before you were dead. Moonstone, real name Zander, who never let anyone touch his hair (everyone knew was a woman's wig) said you didn't die at all, that your head was electrocuted and you were a brain gimp for the rest of your life. But Sepiablush, real name Jane (had nightmares about living in the country) who Moonstone said had already been got to, said nothing at all like that happened. Sepiablush said if you tried to escape maybe The Spark came down and went into you and absorbed you, taking you back up into the sky with it. Divinia, our Spark Intermediary, encouraged these rumours but tempered them by stressing that you would be nowhere near as bright within The Spark as you would if you waited for the time of Bursting Into Flame to begin.

Strike 2

This is the spam mail I got on the Tuesday morning on that day in April when the sun pushed through like it was really serious about spring this year.

Maurice Suckling

-------*Original Message*-------
From: Your future
Sent: 13 April 2004 11.11am
To: Ronan Lynch
Subject: You

Does your present keep obscuring your future?
Is it hard to see it for the dark?
Then you need a spark of light to illuminate the way.
You need The Spark of Divinely Random Intervention.
This is not a cult. It is a lifestyle re-tuning collective.
Follow the link below to light up your future.

I deleted it.

Strike 3

I left university with my degree in the subject I was best at school at, and, gathering about me all my loans, I moved seamlessly into my first badly paid job in advertising. After two years there I moved to a slightly less badly paid job in marketing. After two years there and an affair with Oona, an illegal immigrant who worked in bars in the East End who was always oddly sketchy about her background and never consistent about which part of Eastern Europe she was actually from, I took a job in a telesales company as a recruiter.

The office was in a business park complex in a Might-As-Well-Put-A-Business-Park-Complex-Here part of the city. The campus of box buildings hugged a through-road and broke off from that into square grids. At one end of the main road was a hotel for business people. At the other was a shop selling taste-free sandwiches on large polystyrene style bread, a bank, and a travel agents. There was one large rectangular building with mirrored silver wall-windows and no one knew what it did. My own guess was this was where the Positivity Siphon was housed. Everyday, no matter in what kind of mood you went to work, by mid morning you'd find all your best thoughts and looking forward-tos somehow sapped and you knew for sure it was more to do with where you were than anything about yourself. All your positivity was going, being siphoned off somewhere else – to places you were sure existed, like beaches and places where recumbent sunning people had smiles matched in size by their large glasses of cold white wine.

"Hello, I'm Ronan, I'm calling from Eurocareer Recruitment. Are you looking to make a change? Would you consider yourself an ambitious, well motivated person?"

Two years went by. I dressed in sweatshirts (t-shirts in the summer) and jeans, and I used phones and recruited. I sent emails and recruited. I got up, got on a bus, sat at a desk, recruited, ate my homemade lunch, sat at a desk, recruited, got on a bus, went back home. I was working to pay for my flat I didn't like in a place I didn't like, so I had somewhere to come back to after spending all day doing something I didn't like.

I thought about Roddy and Roxy, my flatmates from university. Roddy was smart but still worked hard. He used to leave trails of half drunk cups of tea round the flat. Roxy was smart, good looking and popular. Sometimes you didn't see her for a week at a time, then she'd return, maybe with a different boyfriend, maybe with a new heartbreak saga. She didn't cook or clean much, but on random occasions when she did she'd cook better than both of us, or clean the flat like we were hoping to sub-let it – taps, bath, cupboards, behind the loo, everything.

Roddy got his first badly paid job in advertising, then got a slightly less badly paid job in advertising, then left and went to live in Estonia. He came back after a year and a half. I heard he did nothing but drink and saved money to come back. Then he got another badly paid job in advertising. I hadn't heard from him since he left.

Roxy left before she finished her course. She was studying Russian, and she'd already done three years out of four. She went travelling, then came back, worked in a bar. Worked in a ski shop, then disappeared. I got a postcard from her last year – sent to my mum's house. I would still take it out of my special shoebox of Things For Keeping and look over it and wonder about her.

Strike 4

Dear Ronan,

Have discovered everything worthwhile.
Know how to make it work. Know how to
make it last. Wish you were here. Please
come and I will explain all.

Then the address was smudged by rain and dirt, the ink had run and I couldn't read it.

Love and anticipation
Roxy

She never wrote again. The front was plain white.

Strike 5

I started having thoughts of tracking Oona down and getting back with her. I could sell all my old university books and CDs, clear the final dregs of my student loans with my savings and we'd get jobs on a farm and live simply, stress free without mobile phones and soap operas on TV, and drink homemade Eastern European wines. I'd grow a large black moustache and she'd wear an apron with nothing else on underneath. We'd make toys for our children out of wood and have humble folk-wisdom style things to say to friends from the old country. I'd learn to slap my thigh heartily if things amused me.

I left a message. She phoned back and we agreed to meet. I started using the internet to search for sites about Eastern Europe and bought a few books – Bulgaria, Montenegro and Rumania were the countries she'd mostly mentioned.

We met in a pub by a canal in North Oxfordshire. We talked about my plan. Oona looked horrified. At first she said she'd forgotten to say, but was actually Polish. When I told her I'd looked briefly into that too her face fell. Her accent suddenly slipped and she confessed her real name was Jessica Brompton, was born in Knightsbridge and went to a private school in Oxford and her parents had houses in London, North Oxfordshire and Monaco. She said Oona Veneva was more interesting.

"So does that mean we're not going then?" I said.

She didn't reply. She just put her tomato juice and Worcester sauce down – which I'd paid for and was only two thirds drunk – got in her black Audi TT and drove off.

I took it as a 'no'.

That was in the October. In the April I got *the* email and deleted it. In the evening I took the bus home. On the empty seat, next to a man I thought for a moment was that big ginger singer out of The Commitments, was a piece of paper. It said:

The Spark of Divinely Random Intervention.
There is a space for you.

I met some friends for a drink. I went home to carry on reading about *The Labbit of Doom*. It was a gripping thriller about a giant half locust, half domestic rabbit that was terrorising the science fiction city of BioStench Nine, and transforming its victims into noisy jumping, computer cable gnawing zombies.

There was a loud clump on the roof of the flat (I was on the top floor) just as the Giant Labbit was cornered by the army and fighter space-ships were about to drop metal netting over it.

I ran to the window to find a parachutist getting to his feet, rolling his chute in. I was thinking of opening the window to say something when I realised he wasn't rolling his chute in, he was laying it out, spreading it onto the pavement. Then I read words:

The Spark of Divinely Random Intervention.
You too can fly.

He saw me looking, raised a hand, slow and steady, then left. I ran downstairs, jumping the stairs in sets of five, but he'd gone. I folded up the chute and carried it back up to my flat. My neighbours looked at me through their blinds and curtains twitched. I put the chute in a cupboard.

The next morning I paid for my bus ticket, only the driver who I didn't recognise, didn't issue me one. Instead the slip of paper said:

The Spark of Divinely Random Intervention.
Are you on-board?

I hesitated, but the doors of the bus had already closed and it was pulling out into the road. I found a spare seat, next to a girl who I thought for a moment was the 80s singing sensation Kate Bush with her enormously big brown eyes. I was half ready for her to start with 'it's me, your Kathy, I've come home, ho-o-o-o-o-o-ome.'

Two heads from the people on the seat behind me, one either side of my face, poked out over my shoulders.

Left head, breath like oranges: "It's not a cult, you know."

Right head, breath like lemons: "It's a lifestyle re-tuning collective."

I started to sit forward on my seat, ready to stand up and get off at the next stop.

Left head, breath like oranges: "Remember Roxy?"

Strike 6

The camp was near a forest somewhere outside Bristol. We were given long white robes. We didn't have to wear them, but mostly people wanted to. After a bit everyone wore them and wouldn't think of wearing anything else, and then, when the bin-bags came round' everyone got rid of their own clothes because they never wore them anymore.

Our tents were in a circle. In the centre was Divinia's tent, a very large, bungalow-sized bright white tent with no markings on it. Even the maker's markings had been removed. As the weeks went by the rings of tents got deeper and deeper. At first the circle was just one tent deep. Within weeks it was four, then five and then six deep. They put wire fences up, to protect us from outsiders and to try and control the numbers of people pouring in. By the time I'd been told I could see Roxy the tents were twelve deep. Except Roxy wasn't Roxy anymore. She was Divinia.

I was told to remove my sandals and passed three large bouncer men in long black robes on the way through. I waited in a chamber of the tent, large enough to stand up in without stooping, and I could have lain down twice over if I'd had more of me to go round.

Divinia rushed through in a streak of white robed light and hugged me hard.

"Rox, Rox, it's brilliant to..."

"Divinia," she said, stepping back, re-settling her robe about her.

"...Yeah...brilliant to see you."

"I'm so pleased you heard the call, Dreamsock."

I still wasn't used to my new name, but I had stopped wincing at it. Names were given. You didn't get to choose them.

"The address was...the ink on the postcard had...I couldn't..."

"Don't worry about it. You got here in the end, didn't you? Well then, don't a worrier be. Remember, part of re-tuning your lifestyle is to disconnect the worry."

"Yes, yes," I said, remembering it word for word now.

"To make it work is human..."

I joined in, "to make it last, divine."

She smiled, though I thought it a slightly glazed smile, as if she were looking a little past me, and thinking back I never remember her smiling that way when we lived together. Not even on many beers nights.

"Do you think the food here acceptable?" she said, surprising me.

Was she kidding? The food was incredible. There were rumours of London chefs being responsible. I hadn't missed a meal since I'd arrived. The menus were always so varied and exciting. Every cuisine I'd ever heard of and every one I hadn't was offered. I used to join the crowd of people every morning to read the day's menu choices.

"Yuhu. It's excellent."

Again, a smile I didn't recognise from our flat sharing days.

"Go now and re-join the collective."

And she made the little striking a match gesture that was our sign for counting down to the day, soon coming, when The Spark would ignite and we would all join together as part of the same bright light when the time of Bursting Into Flame began. I returned the same gesture without thinking and was emerging out of the tent before I'd realised what had happened.

Strike 7

I was happy there. All the time. I liked how I had the same, often newly laundered, long white robe to wear everyday. It made me feel bright and cheery and clean.

The camp continued to grow. There were rumours of more permanent buildings being constructed, and everyone was delighted to hear it because no one could bear to think of leaving.

One morning, taking a walk after breakfast, I recognised Roddy, or Rhythmpencil as he'd been renamed. We talked, and after a while he had to get on his way being happy, and so did I.

The permanent buildings went up rapidly. Large rectangular, functional boxy ones. They hugged a main through-road, then broke off from that into square grids. I was asked to help with recruitment, and I was happy to. I went each day to a building and used the newly installed phones and email system, which made me happy.

"Hello, I'm Dreamsock, I'm calling from The Spark of Divinely Random Intervention. Are you looking to make a change?"

I found it intensely fulfilling and utterly enjoyable work.

More buildings were built, including a hotel at one end of the through-road, and a collection of excellent food places at the other. More people flooded into the camp. This was when the life-style re-tuning collective hit a critical period. The population of several hundred thousand started breaking into rival factions. We had to contend not only with The Randomly Divine Spark of Intervention (charlatans) and The Divinely Intervening Spark of Randomness (opportunists), but also The Spark of Interventionally Divine Randomness (militants), The Random Spark of Interventional Divinity (disorganised), and The Divinely Random Intervening Spark (a cult). As a result I started to work more hours and the offices where I worked became larger: we had more work to do to persuade people to join us instead of any of our rivals. I was extremely happy about this.

Then, one evening, just after tea, having stayed late at work again, which always made me happy, I was walking along the corridor on my way to the loo when I bumped into Oona Veneva, who was really called Jessica Brompton, or should I say Destinyellow.

"Hey...you...what's wrong? You don't look happy."

"She put her fingers to her lips, looked all around her, especially into the corners where the walls met the ceiling, and tugged me outside by the arm.

Whispering right into my ear inside my flat, under the duvet, with the camp radio turned up loud it was hard to hear her at all.

"Don't eat the food. It's drugged."

"But!"

She put a hand over my mouth.

"Would I lie to you?" she said.

I started to make another noise, but her hand clamped down harder on me.

The next morning before breakfast she came round and delivered a small hamper with sandwiches and fruit and a bottle of sparkling water.

Strike 8

"This is Dovetail," said Oona, "or Bruce as we prefer to call him." Bruce nodded, to his left were Flightstar, Moonstone, Sepiablush, and Rhythmpencil, who all nodded in turn, except Roddy who just looked straight at me, before looking away to check no one was outside at the window. Our meetings were held in the basement of the launderette building complex. We met at different times of day and night and never in exactly the same room. We communicated to each other on the times of meetings by leaving twigs in the ground near a tree rumoured to have been imported from Spain, placed near the Robe Repairs complex. One twig in the ground meant a certain meeting room, if it was to the left of the tree at 90 degrees it meant midday, to the right at 90 degrees meant at midnight and so on. We had up to eight pre-designated rooms.

Once I'd stopped eating the food provided it became clear to me that my situation was terrible. I was, in fact, in much the same condition as I had been before I joined the lifestyle re-tuning collective. Except now it was worse because I didn't even have a range of different clothes to change into whilst going about my pointless existence.

"You know the police don't even know this place is here, don't you?" said Oona one night we were together in my flat watching

Divinia talk about The Spark, on the only TV station anyone could tune into.

"Do you think," I whispered, moving my hand onto her knee, "if we ever get out of here we might get to go somewhere together? You know, settle down somewhere. I wouldn't necessarily have to grow a moustache – that was optional…though I was quite keen on you in an apron with nothing else."

I smiled winningly. I know I got it out right. You don't spend half an hour in the morning and half an hour at night practicing winning smiles to not know if you got it out right or not when it counts.

"Did you hear about Flowerlamb?" Oona more mouthed it than whispered.

"No. What?"

"She was caught climbing the Southern Perimeter Fence."

"What happened to her?"

Oona put her fingers to her temples and twisted them, making the brain gimp sign.

I had been a member of The Escape Collective for nearly five months before Oona told me about the tunnel. For the next six I helped dig it with a plastic spoon and the corner of an old school protractor.

Strike 9

The rumours of what happened to caught escapees were already rife. We didn't discuss them much though, since our meetings were short by necessity and focused on the practicalities of escape.

"Change of plan," said Oona, in the basement of one of the hair braid complexes. This was a new venue. In recent weeks all eight of our other meeting rooms had been detected. There were suspicions within the group, but for the most part people believed that the camp guards were getting wise to us. We had twice barely escaped undetected and taken to leaving messages by using pens and pencils and showing them in our top in-trays at work.

"My sources say tomorrow is the Time of Bursting Into Flame."

We all looked from face to face. Expressions hard to read, hiding thoughts all much the same.

"Anyone still here tomorrow will…you know."

"The tunnel's not finished yet," said Rhythmpencil.

"We go tonight," said Oona.

"It's short of the woods," said Flightstar.

"We go tonight," said Oona.

Flame

2.55am exactly we assembled at Oona's room. Her flat was on the ground floor. We lifted the bath up and the tunnel went down from there.

2.56am we began our scramble through the dark, with the sides of the tunnel pressing in on us, like we were pieces of food almost stuck in the throat of the ground. The sides were loosely boarded by spare pieces of wood, but soil still fell as we squeezed and heaved past. After a time you learnt to keep your eyes closed. You could barely see anything anyway. The only light was from Oona's tiny penknife torch up ahead. When you got the feeling that you had to turn back you knew you couldn't because there was someone right behind you, their hands almost touching the soles of your sandals. Instead you internalised it, and just as you were struggling through the airless confines of a narrow dark tunnel, so you imagined your hope, a tiny red dot, struggling, pushing its way through a narrow black tunnel inside your mind. If you thought about the redness of the dot it helped get you through.

We emerged nearly an hour later, the sweat visible on our faces in the dim light from the overcast night, smellable at a greater range.

We started to make our way into the woods, the tunnel had popped us up short of them as predicted, when a spotlight the size of a giant moon suddenly swung onto us, lighting us all up like biology samples on a microscope slide. Then came the shout, and the sirens, the panic and the running, and the heart pounding and adrenalin, and the dogs and the shouting, and the screaming and the yelling and the scrambling and the falling and the running in all directions.

Strike 1

I was among those who got away that night. When we returned with the police the entire building complex was deserted.

I was interviewed by the news and a couple of papers, one of which accused me of making it all up. I always did my best to hide my feelings about Oona not being one of those who had made it out.

I got a job in a recruitment agency in another town. The office was in a business park complex in a Might-As-Well-Put-A-Business-Park-Complex-Here part of the city. The campus of box buildings hugged a through-road and broke off from that into square grids. At one end of the main road was a hotel for business people. At the other end was a shop selling taste-free sandwiches on large polystyrene style bread, a bank, and a travel agents.

"Hello, I'm Ronan, I'm calling from Realcareer Recruitment. Are you looking to make a change?"

Not a day goes by when I don't feel glad I got out the camp, before…you know. The only thing I miss about it, apart from some of the people, is the food.

Everyday I wear a set of clothes conforming to the company dress code (as per section 19.04 sub section 3 of the company manual) and yet make sure that it is, as often as practical, a fresh selection from my own choice of clothes bought from a range of high street retailers I feel I can depend on for both value for money and for the latest styles.

September 12th

'Let us build heaven here,' they said, as they left their ships and stood on the shore of the new world. And they built it out of wood and the people came. And the streets were small and ran with sewage.

'Let us build heaven anew,' they said, and they tore down the wooden hovels and replaced them with brick houses, and the people came. And the streets grew wider and stank of horse manure and ran with the blood of riots and unrest.

'Let us build planes that we may be like the birds and enjoy the sensation of flight and look upon all the world,' they said. And they built planes of wood and they sent them to war.

'Let us build planes anew,' they said, and they built them of metal and the people sat inside them and looked down upon all the world, and that world filled with greenhouse gases from those planes.

'Let us build heaven anew,' they said, and they tore down the brick houses and they built towers of glass, and the people came. And the sun reflected off the towers like pillars of a new world in the sky. And the people below were fighting and killing and thieving. And the people below were gluttons and adulterers, and envious and proud and lazy and lusting.

And the people below looked up as they flew metal planes into the towers of glass. And they saw people jumping. And they saw the fires and the smoke. And they ran as the towers came down and ashes and dust covered them.

And the ashes and dust covered the whole world and people looked on as if the end of the world was come.

'If we cannot build heaven,' they said, 'let us build the idea of it

anew,' and from rubble and dust and shattered lives they began to build it out of the only materials they had left; from words and thoughts and all imaginings.

   And the people came.

THE AMAZING ADVENTURES OF NO ONE IN PARTICULAR

Episode 6

205

...or earlier...

...and I did wish that I'd bought a sandwich I liked...

...and not given it away.

I ate my apple.

Then threw it away on the grass, as you're allowed to in nature.

And I didn't feel as OK as I thought I would.

This was largely, I thought to myself, because I didn't know what to do next.

I could picture myself back in the town...

...back on the train...

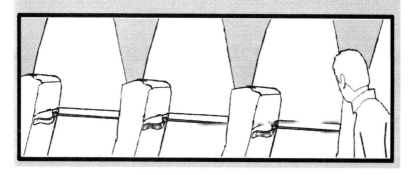
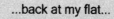

...back at work...

...back at my flat...

...back at the pub.

But I could picture it all so clearly...

...that I didn't seem to need...

...to actually be there.

Or anywhere else.

And as I wondered if all my life would feel like this, I heard the sound of birds flying overhead.

And I watched as they changed
and re-changed formations in
the empty sky.

They folded and re-folded over
each other, like the way an idea
can change...

... and all the other ideas know
how to follow.

And as my eyes followed them into the distance, I wanted to think
they were doing it all for me, just because I
actually was somewhere, if only for now.

This Way For People

I didn't know where I was going to go, but I just knew I had to get out of the office for a while. For once I managed to get away clean without any last minute calls or emails or visitors and stood up from my desk and put my jacket on just as my computer's digital clock in the bottom right hand corner hit bang on 13.00.

I didn't really have a plan. I started walking with the vague idea of getting some lunch. I was only sort of hungry, not yet crossed over into actual hungry, and besides I was all out of ideas as to what I wanted so I didn't head off in the direction of any particular shop. Then I realised I was heading into the high street, and that was bad. Once I got there, I would *be* there, and then I would have to think of somewhere else to go. I decided to take a long cut through a couple of streets I hardly ever went down.

The first of these streets gave me my Show Me Something White feeling. It was an alleyway more than a street. Either side was a dull brick, made duller by the recent rain. One side was the back of a pub, the other the back of a restaurant. There were air con boxes jutting out of both sides. There were puddles on the ground and the sky was that headache inducing smudged slate colour that threatened rain but lacked the guts to go through with it. The bright blue plastic waste bins on wheels, because they were bright and plastic, only added to the feeling. As I came out of that alleyway I saw the markings on the road, the supposed to be yellow of a double yellow line, and the supposed to be white of a parking bay, and the feeling of wanting something really properly white grew.

The next street had a couple of shops on it. A locksmith's and a hi-fi shop. There was a battered dull green door open on one side, a sign in black felt tip on a sheet of weather-beaten white A4 sellotaped to it and flapping in the wind that was whipping up. The handwriting was quite large and there were lots of branches coming off each letter, reminding me of drawings of beanstalks in children's books.

Madame Kana
will read your palm
£10 £11
Palm Reading

The extra £1 bit stuck in my head. Someone had done their finances and worked out that the £1 would make all the difference.

As I walked up the creaking duck egg blue paint flaking staircase I was running through conversations in my head, justifying to myself what I was doing.

Never had it done before. Just wondered what it would be like. £11 isn't much. I'm not saying I believe in it, just thought it would be an interesting way of spending my lunch break. She needed my money.

At the top of the staircase was another sign, in the same handwriting as the one downstairs.

This way for people
⇨

The door was open, so I entered. A large woman with a sofa throw sized black shawl and long black-grey and white streaked hair had her back to me, clicking away at a computer, with what looked like an Internet Explorer logging off screen.

She swivelled round on her black office style chair and faced me, just as I was right in the middle of giving what I think was a guppy fish face.

"Sit down, please," she said, and gestured over to the purpled drape covered sofa in the corner by the table and a wooden chair. Her large arm jangled with the shake of the multiple bracelets along it. She looked like a well-fed Aunt, welcoming and unsettling at the same time.

"Thank you…I saw the sign…is now…?"

"Yes, now is perfectly fine," she said, rearing up and launching her large battleship frame over towards me. The room started to disappear behind her, swallowed up in her wake.

"If we could get the money out of the way then I can concentrate much better," she said.

That's what you'd expect. Fair enough. Makes sense. If this was real should it be related to money?

"Of course."

I handed over the £10 note. Then the £1 coin. A shiny one. A waste of good money.

She reached out and seemed to engulf the money and hide it away somewhere among the dark folds of her shawl.

"Thank you...now, then," she said, and turned on the large bright standing lamp in that corner of the room. The cone of light fell down from almost directly above and it felt instantly warmer. Madame Kana brought the light lower, adjusted its direction a little, and settled herself into the creaking wooden seat opposite me.

"Let's see, then," she said, jutting her hands out quickly, meaning for me to copy her, and I put my palms out face up.

I watched her face as she stared at my hands. I hoped I'd cleaned them properly. I tried to remember what state my nails were in. It certainly looked like she was looking. Her mouth was closed and her lips twitched as she pulled faces to herself.

She pulled out a magnifying glass from somewhere within gulfs of her black clothes and looked some more.

I wondered how much of her must be over the side, on either side of the chair, and decided that she must be sure it holds her weight. She leant forward some more as she appeared to follow a line on my right hand. The chair creaked louder than before, so close to the sound of wood cracking it might even have been that. The chair had to break one day. Today might be that day.

She looked up and met my eyes.

"Have you ever had your palm read before?" she asked.

"No," I said, feeling uneasily as if this sounded rude, or bad, or wrong, or all three.

She turned round and threw a quick look at the clock on the wall above her computer. It was already 13.22. She snapped her head back round and her cheeks kept going a little longer than the rest of her.

Maurice Suckling

"Let's discuss your present first," she said.

"You work in an office, an office nearby. You use a machine, a computer, also, a machine with images – a printer, but something else – we'll come back to that – you had breakfast this morning – toast, or cereal – I'm not very good at food...

"Let's go back to the office – a computer, a printer, a, looks like a...

"Looks like a photocopier – and this looks recent."

She flicked her gaze back along the line she'd been looking at, seemed to shift to somewhere else on my hand, followed that for a time, then went back to this first line.

"You found an image of someone's photocopied hand left in the out tray – a girl's hand – you still have it. You photocopied your own hand and left it. The next day it was gone, and in its place was a photocopy of someone's foot. You still have that too. You photocopied your own foot. The next day that was gone, and in its place was the photocopy of a girl's...A girl's bottom. You kept that as well. You photocopied your bottom, and the next day it was gone. So you sent an email to the girl in the office you thought you'd been exchanging photocopies with – a girl you liked. But the email bounced back and you found out she'd left and gone to work somewhere else. I'm getting a name. The receptionist. A strange name. An X. Xena?" She looked up.

I nodded slowly, thinking I must still have her name in felt tip on the back of my hand from yesterday.

"You have money worries – just sold your music CDs for your credit card bill. You want to work somewhere else – looks like a job application – no, two job applications. Oh dear, that's a shame. Well, we'll come back to the future in a moment."

She looked up, met my eyes, and reminded me of an old primary school teacher.

"Keep going though, love, don't worry."

She took a big breath.

"Now, seat belt on!"

Then she looked straight back down and moved her magnifying glass to another part of my hand, again seeming to move gradually along the length of a line she could see.

"So back, back, back – there's you at school – oh dear, how

embarrassing for you! As I'm sure was that! Though that was probably worse.

"Let's skip ahead a little. And a little bit more. Ah, here we go, graduation photos! And here's you stacking shelves – now a petrol station – aha! Now we've found you and your computer screen!" I felt her look at me but I was looking at the split in the floorboards.

"Let's have a little closer look at this, then!"

The chair creaked again as she shifted forwards on it.

"Feelings of never doing anything, going nowhere, bills, getting up, going to work, working, pointless evening, bills, working, and, oh, that's interesting! Oh."

She blew on my hand and a large speck of blue dust fluttered into the light.

"Sorry, my mistake."

She blew air out the side of her mouth like a workman taking a breather.

"Let's bring things up to date."

"So, there's the photocopier, and the photocopies in the locked desk drawer, the email, the rain, the clock, your jacket, something not white, a shiny £1 coin."

She paused.

"An elegant, voluptuous lady "

She looked back round at the clock. I didn't look to see the time. I just watched her face tightening with concentration. She went back to my hand, and held the rounded bit of my palm by the base of my thumb.

"Let's look ahead, then. Let's look at your future."

She almost winked with her smile as she blew hair from her eyes, rolled her sleeves up, to reveal jangles of bracelets up both arms.

Then she took up both my hands again. She looked between them and seized on a line on my left hand. She moved even closer with her magnifying glass. The chair creaked louder still as she shifted closer. I pulled my hand away a little, my reflexes springing to action in case I needed to try and stop her falling on top of me and smothering me. I could be trapped like that for days and no one would know where I was. If my ribcage survived and I had access to oxygen, dying of thirst would be the most likely cause of death. She pulled my hand back.

"Ah."

"What?" I said, watching her head follow the course of a line so slowly her head barely moved at all.

"I see."

"What? What is it? What's going to happen?"

Then she put the magnifying glass down on the table with a heavy clump, swept both her black wing like arms round me and hugged me tight and full. The bracelets on her arms dug into me all up my back, and I imagined indents not only in my skin but in my bones as well. She pressed me deeper into her, hugging tighter. Then I began holding, holding, not letting go, and I wanted a human to never let go of me again.

More quality fiction from Elastic Press

The Virtual Menagerie	Andrew Hook	SOLD OUT
Open The Box	Andrew Humphrey	£3.00
Second Contact	Gary Couzens	£5.00
Sleepwalkers	Marion Arnott	SOLD OUT
Milo & I	Antony Mann	SOLD OUT
The Alsiso Project	Edited by Andrew Hook	SOLD OUT
Jung's People	Kay Green	SOLD OUT
The Sound of White Ants	Brian Howell	£5.00
Somnambulists	Allen Ashley	SOLD OUT
Angel Road	Steven Savile	SOLD OUT
Visits to the Flea Circus	Nick Jackson	£5.00
The Elastic Book of Numbers	Edited by Allen Ashley	£6.00
The Life To Come	Tim Lees	SOLD OUT
Trailer Park Fairy Tales	Matt Dinniman	SOLD OUT
The English Soil Society	Tim Nickels	£5.99
The Last Days of Johnny North	David Swann	£6.99
The Ephemera	Neil Williamson	£5.99
Unbecoming	Mike O'Driscoll	£6.99
Photocopies of Heaven	Maurice Suckling	£5.99
Extended Play	Edited by Gary Couzens	£6.99

All these books are available at your local bookshop or can be ordered direct from the publisher. Indicate the number of copies required and fill in the form below.

Name_____
(Block letters please)

Address_____

Send to Elastic Press, 85 Gertrude Road, Norwich, Norfolk, NR3 4SG.
Please enclose remittance to the value of the cover price plus: £1.50 for the first book plus 50p per copy for each additional book ordered to cover postage and packing. Applicable in the UK only.

While every effort is made to keep prices low, it is sometimes necessary to increase prices at short notice. Elastic Press reserve the right to show on covers and charge new retail prices which may differ from those advertised in the text or elsewhere.

Want to be kept informed? Keep up to date with Elastic Press titles by writing to the above address, or by visiting www.elasticpress.com and adding your email details to our online mailing list.

Elastic Press: Winner of the British Fantasy Society Best Small Press award 2005

Previously from Elastic Press

Unbecoming by Mike O'Driscoll

Mike O'Driscoll plays with our imagination and expectations. What results is a strangely brewed cocktail of terror: dark, dangerous, and sometimes downright dirty, O'Driscoll's stories get under your skin and into your head, where the freedom to prowl the peripheries of your consciousness becomes addictive. Uncompromising and unflinching, this is modern horror at its very best.

"Identities in crisis, lives falling apart. Wherever Mike O'Driscoll's stories are set the light is fading to a dusky noir but his characters are still recognisable as people you know. Compassion as real as the horror: O'Driscoll doesn't do inauthentic. The monster within is pissed off" – Nicholas Royle

Forthcoming from Elastic Press

So Far, So Near by Mat Coward

In Maurice Suckling's debut collection slices of life react and interact against a consumerist background where expectations of what we are and where we should be going are frequently in conflict with reality. Combining traditional storytelling, vignettes, emails, text messages, and a cartoon, *A collection of succinctly observed events, characters and phenomena which takes a fresh look at the world and our collisions with it* – Dirk Maggs (director of the Hitchhikers Guide to the Galaxy Radio Series)

For further information visit:
www.elasticpress.com

Out Now From Elastic Press

Extended Play:
The Elastic Book of Music

What does music do for you? Is it an art form, mood enhancer, or just something to jump around to? From the orchestra pit to the mosh pit music inspires our lives, is universal and personal, futuristic yet primordial. As the soundtrack trigger to a thousand memories it can be seductive yet soulful, energetic and prophetic. But the immediacy of music has rarely been exploited within literature. Until now...

With fiction from Marion Arnott, Becky Done, Andrew Humphrey, Emma Lee, Tim Nickels, Rosanne Rabinowitz, Philip Raines, Tony Richards, Nels Stanley, and Harvey Welles.

Accompanying the stories, songwriters comment on how fiction has influenced their music, with contributions from JJ Burnel, Gary Lightbody, Chris Stein, Sean "Grasshopper Mackowiak, Lene Lovich, Chris T-T, Rebekah Delgado, Tall Poppies, jof owen, and Iain Ross.

www.elasticpress.com